"We'll get to the bottom of whatever this is. We'll find a way for you to be safe," Dean promised. "I won't leave until we do."

"But what about the kill team?" Kate asked.

"Sitting around waiting for them to arrive is suicide. Pretty much like you handling this on your own."

"It wasn't fair of me to ask you to help. I'm sorry. It was selfish."

"You're concerned about a motherless newborn. That's the opposite of selfish. I'm glad I came back. You needed me." *Still do.*

"It's such a big risk for you to take."

She was worth it.

"I've got some time before that team will get here. I can do a lot of digging in twenty-four hours." But he'd stay longer to ensure she was safe.

"There's so much to figure out and we haven't even had a chance to talk. That's not much time."

No, it wasn't. No time at all when he wanted weeks with her. Months. Years. A lifetime. "I'll make it work."

DISAVOWED IN WYOMING

JUNO RUSHDAN

This one is for my tribe. I couldn't do it without you.

ISBN-13: 978-1-335-48934-0

Disavowed in Wyoming

Copyright © 2021 by Juno Rushdan

For questions and comments about the quality of this book, please contact us at CustomerService@Harlequin.com.

Harlequin Enterprises ULC
22 Adelaide St. West, 41st Floor
Toronto, Ontario M5H 4E3, Canada
www.Harlequin.com

Printed in U.S.A.

Juno Rushdan is the award-winning author of steamy, action-packed romantic thrillers that keep readers on the edge of their seats. She writes about kick-ass heroes and strong heroines fighting for their lives as well as their happily-ever-afters. As a veteran air force intelligence officer, she uses her background supporting Special Forces to craft realistic stories that make readers sweat and swoon. Juno currently lives in the DC area with her patient husband, two rambunctious kids and a spoiled rescue dog. To receive a free book from Juno, sign up for her newsletter at junorushdan.com/mailing-list. Also be sure to follow Juno on BookBub for the latest on sales at bit.ly/BookBubJuno.

Visit the Author Profile page at Harlequin.com.

CAST OF CHARACTERS

Dean Delgado—Disavowed, falsely branded a traitor to his country and in hiding, he's desperate to reconnect with the people he left behind fifteen years ago. Laramie is the last place he thought he'd have to use his lethal skill set, but it makes him the only person who can keep his former lover safe while they unravel a dangerous conspiracy.

Kate Sawyer—Veterinarian and the owner of Loving Paws mobile pet clinic. She's never been able to get over her first love or forgive the way he abandoned her. When violent circumstances bring them face-to-face, she's forced to trust the man who once turned his back on her.

Lucas Delgado—CIA operative and Dean's estranged brother.

Hunter Wright—Former leader of the Topaz Unit. Every member of his rogue team is family to him. The most important thing is clearing their names.

Jim Ames—The local sheriff.

Holden Powell—Deputy sheriff with a long-standing grudge against Kate.

Kelly Russell—CIA deputy director of operations. Her interest in the Topaz Unit is personal as well as professional.

Chapter One

The phone rang, jolting Kate Sawyer awake. She didn't remember falling asleep but must've drifted off after the noise from the bar beneath her apartment had finally died down. She peered at the alarm clock. The red lights blinked 2:23 a.m. Nobody called at this hour with good news.

Bolting upright, she reached out and turned on the light on her nightstand. Her work cell was ringing. Not her personal phone. There was an emergency with a sick or injured animal for someone to call in the middle of the night.

"Loving Paws Mobile Veterinary Services," Kate said, rubbing the sleep from her eyes.

Anything urgent she referred to the local animal hospital. Alpine was the closest and offered 24-7 critical care.

"Help me," a woman said. Her voice was low and tight, thick with emotion.

Kate pushed back the covers and put her bare feet on the carpet. "Ma'am, do you have a wounded pet? If so, Alpine Animal Hospital would be better suited to handle the situation."

Not only did they have an on-call vet available, but

also a technician to assist and any equipment that she might not have at her disposal. She operated out of a twenty-six-foot La Boit truck that consisted of an exam table, a small surgery suite for minor procedures, digital radiology, a hand-held ultrasound and dental equipment. Routine well checks and running basic diagnostics for about fifty patients a month were her bread and butter.

"Please," the woman said in a strained way that unsettled Kate's stomach.

Something horrible must have happened. "What's wrong, ma'am? Can you tell what the problem is?" Was it a poisoning? An intestinal obstruction? Animals ingested things they shouldn't all the time, from chocolate to Legos. If she had more information, she could try to provide some immediate assistance over the phone.

"You have to come now." The woman sucked in a deep, shuddering breath that tugged at Kate's heart.

"Come where?"

"Downstairs," the woman said. "I'm here. Hurry. Please."

The call disconnected.

Kate lurched from the bed and rushed to the window overlooking the private parking area for owners of the street-level businesses and residents of the second-floor apartments. She shoved back the blackout curtain. Lights on the exterior of the building and streetlamps across the road ensured the lot was always well lit. So illuminated it made it difficult to sleep at night. She had a clear line of sight to her mobile pet truck, but she didn't see anyone.

Beside her truck was the Jeep Renegade that belonged to the bartender, Davis Johnson, whom everyone called DJ. Farther down were two other sedans she recognized as her neighbors'.

Scurrying around her bedroom, Kate quickly got dressed, slipped on her sneakers and threw on her lab coat. She grabbed her keys and rushed out the door of her corner apartment.

A cold February breeze slapped her in the face, making her reconsider whether to go back and grab her coat. But there was a hurt animal who needed her right this minute. A poor dog or cat was suffering, could even be bleeding out. No time to waste going back for her jacket.

Wyoming's winters were harsh and bitterly cold, but soon enough she'd take shelter from the elements inside her truck. At least it wasn't snowing.

She raced down the exterior staircase, her feet pounding against the metal steps. As she turned onto the walkway, she stopped short.

In the shadows, a woman was leaning against the brick wall of the bar, bent over...holding her pregnant belly. Wearing a thin dress, a zippered hoodie pulled up over her head, tattered boots and coatless, she must've been freezing. She peered up at Kate. Her face was gaunt, as if she hadn't had a decent meal in a while, and her skin was smudged with grime. She had large blue eyes and pale skin. Kate guessed her to be about nineteen, twenty at the most.

"Dr. Sawyer?" the young woman asked. "You're Kate, right?"

"Yes." Kate had never seen this woman before, but she seemed to know her somehow. If she did, then she should know that Kate was a veterinarian, not an obstetrician. "Are you in labor?"

The woman nodded and sucked in a sharp breath on a contraction as she tightened her frail arms around her midsection. She was so thin that it made her pregnant belly look the size of a watermelon.

Kate hurried to her, wrapping an arm around her shoulder and lifting her from the wall. "Come on. We've got to get you to the hospital."

"No." The young woman recoiled. "No hospitals."

Uneasiness crept between Kate's shoulder blades. "It looks like you're pretty close to having this baby." She got the girl moving and guided her along the walkway toward the truck that she used professionally as well as personally to save on the expense of a second vehicle. "What's your name?"

"Cheryl." Her teeth chattered through bluish lips. She clutched Kate's hand, her bony fingers digging into Kate's. The young woman's skin was ice-cold.

"Listen to me, Cheryl, I have to take you to the emergency room. That's the best place to deliver this baby."

The sudden look of terror on her face punched Kate in the gut. "You can't." Cheryl shook her head. "They'll find me there." She glanced around. "They're looking for me now. We have to get inside."

"Who will find you? Who is looking for you?"

Clenching her teeth, the woman grunted through another contraction. Squeezing Kate's hand, she stopped walking and hunched over in pain. This time her grunt bloomed into a full-blown scream.

The contractions were coming fast, way too fast. Kate estimated less than two minutes apart. Was there even time to get her to the ER?

"I'll call an ambulance." Kate fished her cell phone from her lab coat pocket.

"No hospital," the woman growled, but her eyes,

glazed with fear, reminded Kate of an abused puppy. "Help me or my baby is going to die."

Die?

Who was going to find her at the hospital? Why would anyone want to hurt an innocent child?

All Kate knew for certain was that Cheryl was terrified of something or someone. She had to help this young woman and make sure her baby was delivered safely.

The back door of the bar opened. DJ stuck his head outside and spotted them. "I thought I heard a scream. Is everything okay?"

Kate exhaled in relief, pleased to see him. "No, it's not. Can you give me a hand?"

Without uttering another question, DJ rushed outside to assist them. Kate couldn't think of a better person to help her with this situation—other than an obstetrician.

The older man was well into his late seventies, but his calm disposition—no matter what, even if a bar fight broke out—always put her at ease. Despite the permanent worry lines etched across his forehead and dusting of gray at his temples, he never seemed to fret about anything.

DJ slung one of Cheryl's arms over his shoulders and helped her walk.

"She won't go to a hospital," Kate said, getting closer to her truck.

A gush of fluid splashed to the pavement beneath Cheryl as she groaned, doubling over.

"Her water just broke." Kate tried to quicken their step, but the expectant mother was in so much pain it was difficult for her to walk. "This baby is coming right now."

DJ scooped Cheryl up in his arms in a startling display of strength that belied his elderly frame. He was thick around the middle and didn't appear athletic, but he carried Cheryl to the mobile pet clinic at a pace that had Kate running to keep up.

She fumbled with her keys, looking for the right one. A brutal gust of wind whipped her long blond hair around her face, obstructing her vision. She raked her hair back, angled the keys toward the light and found it.

The harsh hum of a heavy car engine making its way down the road snagged her attention. She stole a glance over her shoulder. Headlights crept along the side street, drawing closer. Whoever was in the vehicle would spot them if they didn't hurry.

She shoved the key into the slot and unlocked it. Swinging the door out, she ushered DJ inside.

He carried the pregnant woman up the three steps as though she weighed nothing.

Hurrying in behind them, Kate closed the door and locked it. She peered through the blinds, scanning the area.

A muscle car, one of those super coupes she'd seen around town, rolled down the street, passing the parking lot, and drove out of sight.

That had been close. She didn't think they'd been seen.

Hoping it was safe, Kate switched on the lights. It was going to be hard enough delivering a baby—she didn't need to complicate the situation by trying to do it in the dark.

"What's going on, Kate?" DJ asked. His voice was deep and scratchy, sounding as weathered as he looked.

"I'm not sure." Her gaze dropped to Cheryl, who was

panting through another contraction. "She says someone is looking for her."

Kate led the way down the narrow aisle to the exam table at the back.

The flat-top metal surface was only forty-eight inches long and not designed for a human, but it was sterile. They'd have to make it work.

She pulled out some supplies from the cabinets. First, she covered the metal table with a blanket for comfort and put a sterile surgical drape on top. "Set her down here."

DJ gently eased Cheryl from his arms onto the table. She pushed her hood back, revealing dishwater-blond hair that was matted to her forehead from perspiration.

Helping the woman into a seated position, Kate put a folded blanket behind her to prop her up. She had never delivered a baby. Assisting with the birth of a calf out at the Sullivan ranch when the local bovine vet had been unavailable was as close as she'd ever come.

Kate had been in the delivery room in Omaha, Nebraska, the day her niece had been born last year. Although her brother-in-law had been at her sister Claire's side, Kate had read *The Birth Partner* cover to cover to prepare.

That was her, a type-A overachiever in everything. So she avoided doing anything impromptu. It only increased the chances of failure.

A flutter of doubt set her nerves on edge. The thought of what rested on her shoulders now—the lives of Cheryl and her soon-to-be-born child—gave her a moment of pause.

"Hey." DJ's voice drew her gaze to his. "You're the sharpest doctor I know. If anyone can do this on the fly, it's you," he said, as though he were a mind reader. "I'll be right here with you every step of the way."

One of the many things she appreciated about DJ was that he always knew the right thing to say at just the right moment to make things better. The perfect bartender. Poured her drinks strong. Listened to her troubles without judgment or trying to fix her problems with unsolicited advice. Knew how to give solid encouragement.

DJ took her hands in his, which were covered in latex gloves as always, due to his obsessive-compulsive disorder regarding germs. "You've got this." His brown eyes searched hers, reflecting a familiar warmth that imbued her with confidence. Then he lifted a hand, cupping her cheek in a manner that felt more flirty than fatherly.

Once again, she found herself thinking that if there hadn't been a forty-year age gap between them, and he wasn't such a germophobe, she would've asked him out on a date months ago. Probably shortly after he'd moved to town.

"Okay?" he said.

"I've got this." Kate nodded, trying to convince herself. She leaped into action, tugging on a pair of sterile gloves, and grabbed some green operating towels.

"Tell me how to help," DJ said.

"Talk to her. Keep her calm," Kate said. "Cheryl, can you put your legs up for me? I need to examine you. See how far dilated you are." A single finger inside the cervix would be one centimeter. Once the cervix was about the size of a cantaloupe or a large bagel, it would be time for her to push.

Kate pulled her long dress back to the top of the young woman's knees and covered her with another surgical drape to give her some privacy.

Extensive bruises covered her legs in various shades that ranged from red-purple to yellowish brown. Some marks looked as if they'd been made by a cord. Cheryl had been beaten.

Did she have an abusive husband or boyfriend after her?

But she'd said *they*. Maybe his family was helping him look for her, but why would they want to hurt an infant?

"I've got to get the baby out." Cheryl grimaced. "Now! I've it get out. It burns! Hurts so much."

DJ took her hand. "You see that sign on the wall?" He pointed to the one that read, Free Belly Rub With Exams. Sorry, Pets Only.

"Focus on the sign," DJ said, "and breathe like this. Hee, hee, hoo." He demonstrated, blowing two short breaths followed by a long one as he made the noises.

"Where did you learn that?" Kate asked.

He shrugged. "Saw it in a movie."

It might have been a tip from a movie, but it worked. Cheryl calmed, her gaze focused on the sign, and her breathing regulated.

DJ had the magic touch.

If only Kate could find an age-appropriate guy like him.

She peered under the surgical drape, prepared to check her cervix, but there was no need. "The baby's head is crowning." That explained Cheryl's urgent feeling to get the baby out. They didn't call crowning the ring of fire for nothing. "We're in the home stretch." In minutes, Cheryl would be holding her newborn. "The next time you feel the need to push, I want you to take a deep breath and slowly release it while you bear down."

Cheryl nodded. Seconds later, she was doing as Kate

had instructed. The young woman let loose a guttural cry as the baby's head slipped out.

"A couple more pushes," Kate said, eager to usher this new life into the world. "Wait for the next contraction."

A loud pop sliced through the air as the lock on the truck door gave way. The door was flung open and banged against the side of the vehicle.

Kate flinched at the sound, her heart jumping into her throat.

Two men burst inside the mobile clinic. Both were big and burly, radiating menace. The first guy had a tattoo of a snake on his neck and a crowbar clenched in his fist.

DJ let go of Cheryl's hand. Turning toward them, he stood defensively, blocking the aisle.

"Give us the girl and that baby, and we'll let you two live," the man with the tattoo said.

Fear flooded Kate. The taste of old pennies suddenly filled her mouth. Fragments of panicked thoughts bombarded her. But her mind snagged on one—the only thing standing in the way of those two thugs was a senior citizen.

There was nowhere for them to run. The only door was blocked. Cheryl couldn't move even if there was some way to escape. And that baby was being delivered right now. What were they going to do?

Violence pulsed off those men. They obviously had no qualms about threatening women and a baby. That made them capable of anything. She sensed it in her bones.

But handing over Cheryl or the child was an unthinkable option. Only over her dead body would those men get their hands on either of them.

Kate shoved aside the panic. If she surrendered to

it, the feeling would consume her. She had to keep a clear head.

Cheryl groaned at the onset of the next contraction and bore down again with another gut-wrenching scream, pushing the baby's shoulder's out.

"We gave you fair warning," the guy with the tattoo said, stalking forward, and dread welled in Kate's chest.

The taller man cracked his knuckles, following his buddy deeper into the truck.

Horrible scenarios raced through her mind, making her light-headed, but she had to focus on helping Cheryl. The young woman needed her, and this baby was coming, one way or another.

The guy with tattoo scowled. "Now we're going to make it painful, old man." He swung the crowbar.

A whoosh prickled her ears as the metal slashed through the air.

"DJ!" Kate said, not wanting him to get hurt.

But the elderly man had ducked, avoiding the blow. Then he popped up lightning fast and launched a fist, punching the bigger guy in the windpipe.

The crowbar clattered to the floor. The man gasped. Falling to his knees, he clutched his throat.

DJ jumped over the man who was in a heap in the aisle and kicked the other one backward.

Cheryl pushed again, and Kate caught the baby in a towel. The umbilical cord was wrapped around its little neck. But thankfully it was loose. Moving quickly, she gently eased the cord over the baby's head.

The sounds of a vicious struggle resonated in the small space. Kate only caught glimpses of the scuffle.

DJ blocked an incoming punch and threw a leg up into the man's groin. The brawny guy doubled over with an *oomph*. DJ grabbed him by his jacket and bulldozed him backward, down the steps and out of the truck.

Kate dried the baby off with a towel. The little one started crying. The sweet sound was reassuring. "Those are some nice, healthy lungs." She handed the baby to Cheryl. "It's a boy. A beautiful boy."

Cheryl clutched the baby close to her chest. "He's so small."

The baby did look premature. Probably caused by malnutrition. But he had a strong pulse and good muscle tone and color.

"He's healthy." Kate tied off the umbilical cord, clamping it.

"She was right," Cheryl said, staring down at the baby. "She told me that you'd help me."

"She? Who?" Kate asked. "Who told you to come to me?"

Metal scraped against the floor as the guy grabbed the crowbar and climbed to his feet. "Give me that baby," he said, rubbing his throat and drawing closer.

Cheryl held the newborn tighter. "Please, don't!"

The young woman's scream, the sound of her fear, jump-started Kate's adrenaline.

She whirled and scoured the shelves for something she could use as a weapon. Desperate to grab anything, her fingers curled around an orthopedic bone saw. She threw the surgical tool at his head.

But he swatted the saw to the floor with the crowbar.

Blind panic threatened to overwhelm her. Why hadn't she taken her purse? Inside it she always carried bear spray.

"Please, Smitty," Cheryl begged. "Let us go. I won't say anything."

Reaching behind her, Kate grabbed the first thing she touched. A stethoscope. She closed her fist around the chest piece and swung, whipping the binaural device through the air, trying to keep him back.

He snatched hold of the tubing and wrenched the stethoscope from her hand, tossing it behind him.

Her first instinct was to protect Cheryl and the baby. She threw herself in front of the mother and child, standing with her arms stretched out to shield them from any blows. To stop this monster from taking them by any means necessary. Punch. Kick. Bite. Anything.

Smitty raised the crowbar, and Kate swallowed the wave of terror that almost choked her.

Movement behind Smitty had the big guy shifting around toward it. DJ leaped up, wrapping the tubing of the stethoscope around his neck and hauled him out of striking distance. The old bartender had crept back onto the truck without making a sound. Silent as a ghost.

The two men wrestled, locked in a tense struggle.

She had to do something to help DJ before that thug maneuvered to hit the old man with the crowbar. A hard enough blow would break his bones.

Frantic, she looked around and spotted a stainless-steel instrument tray. She snatched it from the counter. With the metal clenched in both hands, she charged the man.

Desperation and anger made her strong and wild. She slammed the tray down on Smitty's arm. His head. His shoulder. Anything she could strike.

He knocked her off him, throwing her against the counter, but the crowbar slipped from his thick hand. Someone kicked it, sending the metal bar sliding to the rear of the truck.

She scrambled down the aisle and scooped up the crowbar from the floor. By the time she managed to stand, the man had pulled something from his pocket.

A switchblade glinted in the light.

Before she could run to the front of the truck, before she could swing the crowbar, before she could scream in warning, Smitty plunged the knife into DJ's stomach.

"No!" Kate cried out.

DJ flinched. But he didn't stop fighting, didn't even slow down.

Smitty kept stabbing him. Each strike drove a spear through Kate's own heart.

That animal was killing him.

Smitty swung with his other hand to defend himself from the older man's relentless blows. His open hand struck DJ's face, ripping off skin. The big guy stumbled back, pulling out the knife.

There was no blood. Not on the switchblade. Not on DJ's abdomen. No blood anywhere.

For a second, she doubted her eyes.

Smitty stared down at the skin in his hand. At the *face* that he was holding. "What the hell?"

Kate's gaze flew to DJ. Instead of a wrinkled white man with gray hair, she stared at a Latino face with smooth, deep olive skin, framed by inky curls. But that shock wasn't what made her heart seize.

She knew that handsome face all too well.

Senior citizen DJ, the perfect bartender, was Dean Delgado. Someone she'd thought she'd never see again.

Smitty threw the wrinkled face down and ran out of the truck.

DJ—Dean—looked at her. "Crowbar," he said, holding out his hand. His voice crackled, wavering between the old man's and the real one.

Now she could tell that it was digitized.

"Throw me the crowbar, Kate!"

She snapped her mouth closed once she realized she was gaping and tossed the crowbar to him.

He snatched the piece of metal from the air and took off after Smitty.

There was a roaring in her head that sounded like a giant wave was about to break on top of her, smashing her to pieces. In a way, one already had seconds ago.

She stood there, trembling, her hands shaking, her mind whirling from the violence and shock. But it was the gut punch of seeing *him* that truly left her reeling. She felt as though she were floating. Untethered.

Questions piled up in her head, an avalanche of queries. About Cheryl. About who'd told the pregnant woman that Kate would help. About those men.

About Dean Delgado.

Her first love. Her first heartbreak. Her first everything.

A pang sliced through her chest, and she set her teeth against it. He was alive. Back in Laramie. A bittersweet surprise.

Far more bitter than sweet.

Why was he here after all these years? What was with the disguise?

"Don't…" Cheryl said, pulling Kate from her spiraling thoughts.

She turned and staggered to the new mother's side like she'd just been in a car accident.

Cheryl caught hold of Kate's lab coat and tugged on the pocket. "Don't let them…get the baby," she whispered. A tear surfaced, rolling down Cheryl's cheek before her eyes fluttered closed. Her arms went limp, and her legs dropped, dangling from the sides of the table.

Oh, no. Something was wrong with her.

Kate ensured the baby was in a stable position in the crook of his mother's arm and in no danger of rolling off the table. Then she went to examine Cheryl.

Blood poured from her, running over the edge of the metal surface, dripping to the floor.

Cheryl was hemorrhaging. A number of things could've caused it. Placenta problems. A tear in the cervix or a ruptured blood vessel in the uterus.

I can't lose you now. Stay with me.

If Kate couldn't get the bleeding to stop, the young woman was going to die.

Chapter Two

Dean dashed from the mobile van, leaped over the dead body of the first man he'd taken out and raced after the second scumbag who'd had the audacity to threaten a pregnant woman and a helpless baby.

He was going to kill him when he caught him. Not *if*, but *when*.

Not only would that man come after Cheryl and her baby again, but also he had seen Dean's real face. That made him a threat who needed to be put six feet under.

As the would-be kidnapper reached his muscle car, he slowed and patted his pockets. Then he glanced over his shoulder at Dean and kept running.

No keys. They must have been on his buddy. Smitty's bad luck.

Fate was practically gift wrapping this guy for Dean, and he was never one to look a gift horse in the mouth.

The guy rounded the corner of the building and fled out of sight.

A problem that Dean quickly remedied by running at a full sprint.

Tearing around the corner, he spotted the man bolting down the sidewalk. The long side street was deserted.

Quiet, aside from the sound of their pounding footfalls against the pavement.

The crisp night air sharpened his focus, helping Dean strategize how best to kill him. He couldn't beat the guy to death with the crowbar. It had to look like an accident. Self-defense.

Assassination was his specialty, or it had been when he was active with the CIA. A skill he'd hoped to have no use for while hiding out in Laramie. Killing was not something he took pleasure in. The marines had showed him that he was very good at it, and the CIA had cultivated that talent. Taught him to elevate it to an art form.

Not once had he orchestrated *Giselle* or *Swan Lake*. But every job had been calculated perfection.

Except the last one, which had gone awry. A full-blown fiasco that had landed him in a world of trouble. Had him literally and figuratively on the run.

Dean was closing the gap between himself and Smitty, like a heat-seeking missile ready to destroy. His mind was calm. He was driven. Bristling with clear purpose. A few more feet and he'd have him.

Casting a frantic glance over his shoulder, Smitty ran wildly, panicked, straight out into the street.

Tires squealed as a pickup truck plowed into the guy. Metal hit flesh and bone with a sickening thud. Smitty's body bounced into the air, flipped, then landed against the pavement. His neck and left leg were at bad, unnatural angles. Both broken.

There was no escaping fate.

The driver of the pickup truck was a middle-aged guy. Frozen in shock, he had one hand locked on the steering wheel and the other wrapped around a beer bottle. He stared out the windshield, stricken.

The accident couldn't have been more flawless if Dean had planned it.

He peered around, scanning up and down Third Street and Main Avenue. Not another soul in sight. No bystanders to worry about. He spun on his heel before the driver got a good look at him, but when he did, he realized exactly which corner, bathed in light, that he was standing on.

The only one in the small town that had full closed-circuit TV coverage from multiple angles.

A sliver of ice shot down his spine.

Lowering his head, he slipped out of the light, sinking into the shadows as nothing more than a looming specter. But in his gut, he knew it was too late. His real face had been captured on CCTV.

He was a hundred percent certain.

Dean made a beeline back to the parking lot behind the bar. A tingle of awful possibilities crept over his skin.

Local law enforcement wasn't his concern. He wasn't hiding from the cops.

The CIA had put him on a termination list, right along with every other member of Team Topaz. They would be running a facial recognition program that used the most sophisticated algorithms to search for a match from anything an analyst could tap into. ATM security cameras, photos posted online, smart technology video surveillance doorbells and, the most ubiquitous of all, CCTV footage.

Fate was laughing at *him* now. No escaping it. There wasn't a damn thing he could do besides grab his go-bag and run. Again.

The smart thing for him to do was hop in his Jeep,

clear out his long-term room at the motel and hit the road ASAP. But...

Kate.

She knew the truth, that he wasn't seventy-seven-year-old Davis Johnson, bartender extraordinaire, who made all the time in the world to lend her his ear and gave her drinks on the house just because. Cheryl was another factor. The girl might have seen his face, too. But perhaps the help he'd provided would buy the new mother's silence.

Kate was a different matter.

The thought of facing her, fielding questions that he couldn't answer, made his stomach churn. What was he going to say? What explanation could he offer that she would understand, much less one that she'd accept?

A dark haze of anxiety swirled inside him. He stared at the Loving Paws truck, and on the next breath, his gaze swung to his Jeep.

Simply disappearing with no explanations given would be easier. But then history would repeat itself.

Easy wasn't always best, he'd learned the hard way.

A lifetime ago he'd been the biggest jerk and had made the worst mistake by leaving without saying good-bye to anyone. At the time, he had no clue the devastation that would follow in the wake of his absence. But now he had some inkling of what those he'd left behind had been through. His mother. His brother, Lucas. Kate.

The first giveaway had been the fact that Lucas refused to speak to him. Treated him as though they were strangers. Never made eye contact if they happened to pass each other in the halls of the CIA. Never uttered a word after their first encounter at Langley when he'd gone up to his little brother, excited, surprised to see him.

"Lucas, what are you doing here?" Dean had asked, noting he wasn't wearing a visitor's badge but had bona fide credentials. "How long have you been working here?"

"I'm sorry, do I know you?"

Dean had rocked back on his heels, thinking time hadn't changed him that much. "It's me. Your brother."

"I don't know you," Lucas had said with a deadpan expression. "You've mistaken me for someone else. I used to have a brother, but he died."

The words had been a knife to Dean's heart. Once they'd been best friends, as close as brothers could be, and Dean had ruined it.

The second clue had been more insightful, but still vague. One night Kate had had too many drinks, and after the right kind of prompting, she'd spoken his name. Then her eyes had filled with tears. She'd hurried out of the bar, running as though she had been chased by a ghost.

Exactly what the people he loved most in the world had endured escaped him. But it had been painful. Dark.

Only a heartless SOB could take off, disappearing on her twice.

In the moment, Dean made a choice, regardless of the consequences. He ran up the steps of the truck, shutting the door behind him, and scooped up his mask from the floor.

"Call 911!" Kate said, drawing his gaze. She was working feverishly on Cheryl. Blood covered the table and the floor. "She's hemorrhaging and I can't stop it. We need an ambulance. I'm losing her."

He whipped out his cell phone. Made the call. Listened to the operator.

"Laramie 911, police, fire and medical. What's your emergency?"

"Yes, there's been…" His voice fluctuated between the real one and the altered one from the modulator on his throat. He pressed on the tiny piece of equipment. "We need an ambulance," he said, his tone holding steady. "A woman has given birth, but she's bleeding out." The hemorrhage was severe. The young woman had already lost too much blood to save her, but he wasn't going to say anything to Kate. "Come to the Loving Paws mobile pet clinic parked behind Delgado's Bar on Third Street." He thought of the body outside in the parking lot and the other one in the street. "She was attacked by two men. All of us were. But they're dead. Please, hurry." He hung up before the operator could ask any questions or eat up precious time keeping him on the line. "I'll be right back," he said to Kate.

"Where are you going? Help me!"

There was nothing more anyone could do for Cheryl. She wasn't going to make it.

"I'll be back." Turning, Dean jumped down the steps of the truck and bolted for the bar. He started a timer on his wristwatch.

Three minutes. That's how long it would take for the ambulance to arrive. The sheriff's office was right down Main Avenue. Someone from there would show up around the same time. Unless whoever was on duty got caught up handling the car accident first.

He flung open the back door to his family's bar, hustled inside and made his way to the office, where he kept an emergency kit in his sling bag.

Darting into the private bathroom, he fished out the kit. He unzipped it and dropped the bag on the countertop. First, he shed the soiled gloves, tossing them in the trash bin. Germs didn't faze him. The only thing he was fanatical about was leaving his fingerprints behind. Not to mention, applying latex skin on one's hands was tricky. Too many opportunities for tears, particularly while tending bar. Gloves made better sense, far more practical.

He touched up what he could on the foam latex skin on his throat with a topical glue for adhering makeup components to skin. But when Smitty had yanked off his disguise, the fake layer on the throat had been ripped and the voice modulator damaged. They were beyond seamless repair here in the bar with limited time.

A rush patch job was the best he could do under the circumstances. He glanced at his watch for a quick time check. One minute fifty seconds left.

He tugged on the hyperrealistic face mask. The state-of-the-art material had been specially designed and fitted for him courtesy of the CIA and what their deep black budget could afford. On certain missions, it had come in handy to alter his appearance to get close to a target. Looking in the mirror, Dean massaged the lifelike skin, molding the foam to the contours of his face. Special care had to be taken around the eye area. It was delicate and the easiest place to spot that he was wearing a mask. That's why he'd chosen the face of an older man. Wrinkles helped hide the flaws, and people always underestimated the potential physical prowess of a senior citizen.

This face allowed him to blend in, disappear into the background. To be easily dismissed.

It had also almost prevented him from getting the job at the bar.

His dad and stepfather were dead, and his mother was in a nursing home with middle-stage Alzheimer's. A cousin, who had relocated from Fort Collins, managed Delgado's, but she hated the environment, working late nights and had put her private psychotherapy practice on hold. Dean had waltzed in as DJ, claiming to be an old family friend, dishing details only an insider would be privy to, and offered to take the job at half the salary if he were paid under the table. The only stickler was he had to prove he had the stamina for the long hours and the ability to quash a bar fight without too much damage to the property or to himself.

The first few days on the job, his latex gloves had drawn stares and whispers. After he continually mentioned the longtime judge on *America's Got Talent* and an old television show about a detective who both had contamination OCD, the stares had dwindled and the whispers had faded.

Now all his hard work was down the drain.

Sirens wailed in the distance, the approaching sound ticking up his pulse. They would be here any moment. He stared at the obvious jagged tear along his throat and drew in a deep, steady breath. Remained calm. Didn't panic, not ever.

Panicking got people killed.

Digging into his bag, he found a tubular sports bandanna. It was versatile, could be worn as a neck gaiter, face mask, balaclava. Like a loaded gun and a med kit, he found it handy never to leave home without one.

His timer beeped.

He slipped on the stretchy bandanna, concealing the damage to the foam skin around his neck, but the only way to get the voice modulator to function properly was to press down on it while he spoke. Although it wasn't an ideal situation, it was a manageable one.

Sirens blared, drawing closer.

His shirt was slashed through. The midsection was practically in tatters. If not for the silicone false belly he wore to disguise his athletic build, he would have taken a knife to the stomach several times. He hadn't seen Smitty draw the switchblade. The thick, fake paunch had saved his life.

For good measure, Dean changed his shirt, putting on a fresh flannel button-down and tucking it in his jeans.

A loud whoop announced the arrival of the ambulance.

He tugged on two pairs of fresh gloves. Always two. Quickly, he wiped down anything he might've touched with his bare hands. He hurried from the bathroom, switched off lights, threw on his sheepskin leather bomber and locked up the place.

Flashing lights painted the mobile truck an eerie color. He squinted against the harsh glare.

EMTs were loading Cheryl into the back of the ambulance. A sheet covered her face. She was dead.

Such a pity.

Kate must have been devastated to lose her, and now that newborn was motherless.

Holding the baby, who was wrapped in a towel and blanket, Kate stood, talking to Sheriff Jim Ames. Just shy of six feet tall and broad shouldered, the man had a tough yet pleasant disposition. He carried himself like a man in charge, even out of uniform, but he was never arrogant or overbearing the way some of his deputies could be.

With his bag slung over his shoulder, DJ approached

slowly, trying to pick up on the conversation and gauge what he could from the sheriff's body language.

"I did what I could for her to stop the bleeding," Kate said, clutching the baby to her chest and rocking him.

"Then you called 911?" the sheriff asked.

"No. DJ did."

The sheriff spotted Dean coming and redirected his attention to him. Kate's gaze followed. "Evening, DJ," Jim Ames called out when he got close enough for him to greet Dean without yelling.

Dean tipped his head at him. "Sheriff."

Their interaction over the past few months had been limited and casual. Only in passing. Jim struck him as a hardworking, reasonable man. The sheriff never came into the bar for a drink, and during their run-ins on the street he'd never harassed Dean by playing twenty questions with the newcomer. Unlike the deputies. But Laramie was a small, tight-knit community, so it was to be somewhat expected.

"Rough night?" Jim's face might have taken on a sympathetic look, but the sheriff maintained that wary appraisal in his eyes.

Dean gave an affirmative shrug.

"You're responsible for that?" the sheriff asked, hiking a thumb over at the dead body.

Pretending to rub his throat, Dean pushed on the voice modulator. "Yeah. Not sure how I did it, though. Guess I got lucky."

"Some kind of luck." The sheriff looked him over from head to toe and back up again. "She says you chased after the second man. There's another fella a block over. Ran out into the street. Deputy Powell is getting details now from the driver who hit him. Would that be the other assailant?"

"Yep." Dean nodded wearily. "Thought for sure he'd get away. He was so fast."

"Got lucky twice, huh?"

"A fluky coincidence."

"That's one explanation. Certainly odd. In my experience when there's a coincidence, it's better to examine it. Not ignore it." The sheriff assessed him for a long, uncomfortable moment. "Where were you just now and why did you leave the mobile clinic?"

Kate shivered as she made sure the baby was protected from the cold and wind, shielded by the heavy wool blanket.

Dean took off his jacket and draped it around Kate's shoulders. "I went to the bar. To grab my keys."

"Why did you need your keys?"

The quicker to get the hell out of Dodge. But Dean couldn't say anything to make him look as though he'd given the situation serious thought. Normal people didn't plot and strategize in emergencies.

Dean shook his head and gave another shrug. "Not really sure," he said, pressing on the modulator. "A lot happened pretty fast. Figured I might need them."

"Did you get injured in the altercation?" the sheriff asked.

Frigid wind cut through Dean's clothes. January and February were the coldest months of the year in Wyoming, but an Arctic blast had frozen Laramie solid. He clenched his jaw, swallowing a groan. "I'm a bit banged up, but I'll live."

"Is your throat all right?" Jim gestured at his neck. "You keep rubbing it, like it hurts."

Bunching his shoulders against the cold, Dean coughed. "I got hit a few times, but with all the exertion, my throat's dry and little irritated."

Kate's gaze bounced between them. "Yeah, I was worried about him. It was awful." Her voice was so fast and fluttery that Dean suspected she was teetering on a tightrope of emotions. "He took a terrible beating all right, and one of those guys punched him in the throat."

Dean glanced at her for a heartbeat, refusing to let a grimace surface, keeping his face impassive. Why on earth had she said that?

The best lie was a vague one. He shifted his focus back to Jim Ames.

"Is that so?" Crow's-feet deepened as the sheriff's eyes narrowed on Dean. "You took a punch to the throat and still managed to kill one assailant and chase after the other?"

Her eyes flashed wide as the realization of her mistake became clear on Kate's face. Thankfully the sheriff was staring at Dean and not her.

"The blow to my throat sounds a lot worse than it was." Dean coughed again. "I just need some water. Rest. Really, that's all."

"We're ready to go," the EMT called from the ambulance. "We need to take the baby with us."

"I don't want to leave him." Kate shook her head. "His mother was worried about his safety. Can I ride along? To make certain he's okay?"

"Sure," the EMT said with a nod. "I don't see why not. You did help bring him into this world, after all."

Kate looked at Dean like she was reluctant to leave him.

"I'll meet you there," he said, reassuring her that he

wouldn't simply take off. "And drive you back when you're ready."

"Okay." She nodded and turned to the sheriff. "Can we finish this later?"

"Sure, Katie," he said, using the nickname for a little girl. "Get that kid and yourself out of the cold." He waved her off.

Dean watched her climb into the back of the ambulance while the sheriff looked around at the crime scene. The ambulance doors closed, and the emergency vehicle pulled out of the lot.

"Something about this isn't adding up for me," Jim said, studying Dean once more. "Why don't you run me through what happened?"

On a deep shiver, Dean let out a long, hard exhale, and his breath crystallized in the frigid air between him and the sheriff. "I'm freezing. I should get to the hospital, too. Can this wait?" All he needed was a couple of hours. Enough time to talk to Kate, give them both the closure that had been fifteen years in the making. Then he'd hit the road and disappear for good.

"No problem," the sheriff said. "I'll follow you to the hospital. We can finish talking there. It's probably a good idea if a doctor gives you a full, thorough exam, to be sure there are no internal injuries. And we'll get pictures of any bruises for the report."

A physical examination was at the top of Dean's immediate *not-to-do* list. There was no way to avoid discovery under the probing hands of a doctor. "Sure, Sheriff." He gave an easy nod. "Whatever you think is best."

One way or another—*no matter what it took*—Dean was leaving Laramie tonight.

Chapter Three

Reluctant to let go of the baby, Kate handed him to Ellen Fossey, a nurse in the maternity ward on the third floor of the hospital. "You don't understand. There were these men who wanted to take him."

Smitty and his buddy were dead, but Kate didn't know why they had been after Cheryl and wanted the baby. Did the danger end with those two, or had they been a part of something bigger? Had they meant to do harm to a newborn?

Without any solid facts, other than Cheryl's undeniable fear before she died, all Kate had to rely on was the unsettling feeling still tying her stomach into knots.

"Don't worry," Ellen said, offering a gentle smile, "he'll be safe. There are several nurses on duty each shift, and we have security guards and cameras." She gestured to a couple.

Surveillance cameras with tiny red lights hung in a multitude of corners in the nursery and hallway. A security guard came around the corner and stopped at the nurses' station, which faced the elevator, and spoke to a woman wearing pink scrubs.

It should have alleviated Kate's concerns, but she sensed there had been more to Cheryl's troubles. Then there was the mysterious woman who had told the expectant mother that Kate would help her.

Every nerve ending burned with the certainty that the infant wasn't safe.

"We're going to take excellent care of him," Ellen said in a reassuring tone. She was about the same age as Kate. They'd been a couple of years apart in high school, with Ellen being older. Although they were friendly, they'd never become more than casual acquaintances. Back in school, Ellen had always been the first to protect a target of bullying or offer encouragement to others. She had a reputation for being the best neonatal nurse in town. "I'll get him cleaned up, and then the doctor will take a look at him."

"Okay." Kate took a step back. What other choice did she have? She wasn't the parent or legal guardian and had absolutely no say regarding the child.

She stood in the hall and watched through the large nursery window as Ellen gave the baby a sponge bath, put a diaper on him and swaddled him in a warm blanket.

The baby was in the best, safest place he could be at the moment. The nurse at the reception desk had already called Child Protective Services, and now the sheriff was aware of the situation.

Maybe Kate was being paranoid. Her basic instinct to protect the innocent was on overdrive. Or perhaps it was something else, another deep-rooted impulse fueled by her desire to be a mother herself one day. A longing she doubted that would ever be fulfilled.

She pressed her face against the soft sheepskin collar of Dean's jacket and inhaled the smell of him. Woodsy and earthy. Natural. Not some artificial scent from aftershave or cologne. The unique male essence that was pure Dean. Her muscles loosened in response, relaxing, all but the one pumping blood in her chest. Her heart clenched. The scent of him hadn't changed. He still smelled strong and safe.

Tears stung her eyes. The snapshot of him standing in the mobile clinic with his real face exposed was burned into her mind. She didn't want to dredge up the past, but with each breath, every lungful, it was the only thing she could think of.

The elevator chimed, and the doors opened. Sheriff Jim Ames stepped off alongside Dean, disguised as DJ.

Her heart squeezed, thinking about the face hidden beneath that disarmingly deceptive mask. A face she hadn't seen for fifteen years before tonight. Had dreamed of more times than she could count until she had forced herself to stop thinking of him. A bad habit that she'd had to break.

He had been right in front of her for the past seven months. No, almost nine. Pretending to be her friend, joking with her, laughing with her, flirting with her. Listening to her ramble on about everything that weighed on her heart. Things no one else in town knew. About the struggling business she'd taken over from Doc Fitzsimmons when he retired and how she was having a hard time making ends meet. About her happiness for her younger sister, and Claire's perfect life, that sometimes skewed toward envy. To her shame.

And all about her darkest secret… Tyler.

Telling her friendly neighborhood bartender had been akin to sharing with her pastor. But what Dean had done felt like a violation. The depths of his deception made her chest burn.

If the sheriff hadn't been with him, she would've slapped the mask right off his face.

Taking deep breaths, she did what she'd learned to do to endure his disappearance. She compartmentalized. She shoved her feelings, the memories of the past and thoughts of Dean's glaring deceit deep down. Put everything in neat little boxes to be dealt with at a more appropriate time.

"How's the baby?" Dean asked in that fake voice.

"Healthy, I think." She looked back into the nursery. "The doctor's examining him now, and one of the nurses called Child Protective Services."

"That's good," Jim said. "They'll put him in the system, then they'll be able to help me track down the mother's family after we identify her." He touched something attached to his duty belt. A digital recorder. "Katie, did the woman give you her last name?"

Only her parents, her pastor and Jim called her Katie. Though the sheriff wasn't quite as old as they were, she guessed he was in his late forties. He had one kid in college, and the other was a senior in high school. Everything about him was strong yet appealing, from the features on his rugged face to his muscular build, which he'd retained from his days as the star quarterback for the Plainsmen. She appreciated his commanding presence that anchored the town.

"No," Kate said. "Just her first name, Cheryl."

Jim removed his stiff campaign hat, a brown Stetson, exposing his thick, dark hair. Only his lightly silver-flecked sideburns betrayed his age. "Did she mention who those two men were? Why they were after her? Whether one of them might have been the father?"

"I'm afraid not. She didn't tell me anything." But Kate

wished that Cheryl had given her some information to go on, the smallest tidbit that might help protect her son. "I have no idea why they were after her or the baby. I suppose one of them could've been the father."

"I'll have the nurse get a cheek swab," Jim said, "and I'll run it against the DNA of the two assailants. If we get half as lucky as DJ has been tonight, one of those fellas will be a match."

Kate squirmed inside in her skin, trying not to let it show. Jim suspected something about Dean. Her days of loving him and watching out for him were long done. He'd packed his things, dropped out of school and walked away from his family and her. No note. No email. No phone call.

The worst part was that she'd been so hopelessly in love with him that if he'd confided in her, she would've gone with him.

Even though she should be over it, he haunted her. She missed him so much that at times her heart still ached, but there was no way she was ever falling back into the bad habit of Dean Delgado. Getting burned once was more than enough for a lifetime.

Still, no matter how furious she was at him, the instinct to protect him was strong as ever. "You should probably speak with Ellen now," Kate said to the sheriff, hoping to redirect his attention. "It'll be easier to get a cheek swab while the doctor is examining the baby. Once he's finished, they'll feed him and he'll probably fall asleep. You won't want to disturb the little guy then, will you?"

"I hadn't considered that." Jim hit the recorder on his belt, stopping it. "It's been so long since my boys were in diapers. I'll go take care of it, and I'll be right back."

They both nodded.

The sheriff walked a few feet away, a discreet distance, poked his head inside the nursery and spoke with the doctor.

Dean clutched her forearm. "Kate." His voice was a whisper, but the intimacy in the way he spoke her name roared through her.

"Not now," she interrupted, struggling to stem the emotion welling in her chest. Any explanation he offered would only upset her, and getting in a dither in front of the sheriff wouldn't help matters.

"He wants me to get a medical exam," Dean said, and her gaze flew to him. "That can't happen, for obvious reasons." He looked around. "Stall the sheriff for me."

"What? Why?" Her skin prickled. "How am I supposed do that?"

"You're clever. You'll think of something." Dean crossed the hall, casual as he pleased, and ducked into a bathroom.

Who in the heck did he think he was? Slipping into the bathroom to do only goodness knew what while leaving her to cover for him. Assuming that she would. *The nerve.*

Jim closed the nursery room door and turned toward her. His gaze darted about, no doubt in search of Dean, as he came back to stand in front of her. "Where's DJ?"

"The bathroom. I'm sure he'll only be a moment." She grasped the edges of the jacket draped around her to keep from fidgeting. "I'm glad you were on duty tonight to handle this." It was true. She didn't care for Chief Deputy Holden Powell anymore. He used to be a nice guy, but somewhere over the years he'd turned into an arrogant, pushy jerk. And he was one of her exes. A rebound after

Dean had left town. The first in a long line of mistakes in her effort to forget her first love. Tyler had been the last. "Taking the occasional night shift must be tough."

"It's only tough when people start dying. Thankfully that's rare. Tomorrow was supposed to be my day off, so I could get back on a day schedule. But with everything that's happened, I'll be in the office in the morning for sure."

Kate chewed on her lower lip, thinking of how to change the conversation until Dean reemerged. "How's your son Colton doing?"

"Connecticut agrees with him. He loves Yale and has been getting good grades. Maggie and I are so proud of him. Plainsman to Yalie. But," he said, his eyebrows lowered in a grimace, "it's expensive."

"Tell me about it. I'm still paying off my student loans." She was drowning in debt and hadn't even gone to an Ivy League school. Rather than take on Doc's business, she should've left Laramie and started over with nothing, no remnants, no mementos. Moved to a larger city out of state. Maybe Denver, far from the constant reminders of the past that plagued her. Worked at someone else's practice for a few years, established financial security.

A fresh start would have done her good, if one had been possible. The only problem was she didn't know how to lose the baggage she carried in her soul.

"Depending on where our youngest decides to go," Jim said, "we might have to take out a second mortgage on the house."

"I can think of worse concerns for a parent." Concerns Cheryl would never get the chance to have. She looked back at the precious newborn. What was going to happen to him?

The doctor pushed through the door of the nursery and handed Jim a cotton swab sealed in a plastic bag. "Be sure to let us know if you find anything."

"Will do." Jim stuffed the swab in his inner jacket pocket. "How long will he have to stay here until he's released to CPS?"

"Three days if all his tests check out."

Jim gave a nod, and the doctor left.

"How long to run his DNA to see if it matches either man?" Kate asked.

"About the same amount of time," Jim said. "Maybe two, but if the lab is behind, it can take as long as five."

The bathroom door squeaked open. Dean trudged out into the hall and made his way up to them as though exhausted.

He was one hell of an actor. She'd give him that, but she wondered what he'd been doing in the bathroom all that time.

Jim tapped his recorder, starting it up again. "DJ, let me get your basic information and then I'll take your statement."

"Of course." Dean rattled off a full name, someone's date of birth, a phone number and a motel room as an address.

"Can you go through what happened for me?"

"I was getting ready to lock up the bar when I heard a woman scream outside," Dean said, rubbing his throat. "I went to take a look. Saw Kate and Cheryl. Offered to help. We got into the mobile pet clinic. As the baby came, those two thugs showed up. There was a scuffle, and then I don't really remember. It all happened so fast."

Jim's gaze sharpened. "I understand, but I need you to take your time and try to recall as many details as possible," he said, in a calm, patient voice. "The more details—" The squawk of the sheriff's radio hooked on his tan shirt cut him off.

"Sheriff, it's Holden," the male voice on the other end of the radio said. "We just got a call about a break-in in progress at Nelson's Gun and Outdoor Sports shop. I'm leaving the scene of the car accident with the driver handcuffed in the back of my cruiser to respond, but I could use backup."

"On my way," Jim said and keyed off the radio. "It must be a full moon or something." He raked back his hair and put his campaign hat on. "Why don't you two get some rest and swing by my office tomorrow to finish your statements? Oh, and DJ, you should get checked out by a doctor."

"I'm fine, really, Sheriff. The evening wiped me out and I want to get Kate home, but I'll take care of it tomorrow. Scout's honor."

"Okay." Jim tipped his hat at Kate and hurried down the hall.

Once he hopped in the elevator and the doors closed, she spun on Dean. "You were never a Boy Scout."

He shrugged. "I only said it for effect."

"What have you become? Some kind of a pathological liar?"

"My gift for lying isn't pathological, it's professional."

"Huh? What are you, a lawyer hiding out from the mob?"

Dean took her by the elbow and hauled her into the hallway bathroom.

Inside, she yanked her arm free of his grip.

He locked the door. "Look, I know I owe you an explanation. And an apology."

The apology was so long overdue she couldn't care less about it, but the explanation she wanted. "Start talking, and if you ever cared about me, even a little, please, no more lies."

"Of course I cared about you," he said, and she rolled her eyes. "How could you doubt that?"

How could she not?

"What's with the disguise?" she demanded.

"I am hiding out, but not from the mob."

"Then from who?"

"You asked me not to lie, so let's leave it at that. Telling you would only endanger you."

"Are you kidding me?" she asked, poking him in the chest. "You creep into town after fifteen years of turning your back on everything and everyone here—" she poked him again for good measure "—wearing this getup, and you expect me to swallow half-baked truths with no substance? You really never cared about me at all if you think that's what I deserve. What was I to you? A distraction, something to help you pass the time? A plaything you could toss away without a second thought?" She turned on her heel, unlocked the door and opened it to leave.

Dean slammed the door closed. "Please." The supplication in his voice made her pause.

"Please what?" she snapped. "Listen to your baloney and nod my head in sympathy like a good little *ignorant* accomplice? I don't think so." She grabbed the doorknob and twisted it.

Dean slapped a gloved palm to the door and shoved his foot up against it. "Give me ten minutes."

She sucked in a strained breath. "Only if you promise to give me the whole truth."

Clenching his jaw, he shook his head. "When they come looking for me, I don't want you getting caught in the middle, used as a pawn or hurt because you know too much."

Didn't he understand that no one could hurt her as deeply as he had? Not even if they tortured her slowly for days.

"I don't care what kind of trouble you're in." She wasn't concerned for her safety. At this point, she cared more about her sanity and hearing something that made sense. "But I need to know what *it* is." What would drive him to such lengths. Putting on a costume and pretending to be someone else, every day for nine months. The attention to detail, the self-discipline that required boggled her mind. "I've always kept your secrets. You can trust me."

He cocked his head to the side. "That's not entirely true… Is it?"

She recoiled. "What are you talking about?" Not once had she betrayed his confidence. "I would never."

"You're the only person I told what I wanted to be one day." His eyes were cool and unblinking.

Had she told someone?

Kate racked her brain. After he'd taken off, his parents and the sheriff had interrogated her, and she'd given them nothing. Because she'd known nothing. Dean hadn't shared his plan.

It wasn't until years later, at his stepfather's funeral, that his mother had admitted to Kate that she'd received a letter from the marines, congratulating them on Dean's completion of basic training. His mother had burned it, not wanting to upset her husband, but she had been re-lieved to know her son was alive and well.

Growing up together and later while they'd dated, not once had Dean mentioned the military to Kate. Only about becoming a CIA operative. To be an American version of James Bond.

She'd never taken him seriously and certainly had told no one except…

"You mean the CIA?" she asked.

"You told Lucas."

She'd been a senior and Lucas a sophomore. The two of them heartbroken and alone, they'd bonded over Dean. Became close friends. Inseparable. Lucas had even en-couraged her to date Holden in a futile effort to purge Dean from her system.

"I guess it slipped one day," she said. "We only had each other after you abandoned us. But it was your brother, for goodness' sakes—that doesn't count."

"He found me. Did you know that?"

"What? How?"

"He joined the CIA."

The words hung in the air between them, sucking all the oxygen from the room. Light-headed, she suddenly couldn't breathe. Lucas had found Dean and didn't put her out of her misery by telling her where he was, what he was doing. That he was okay.

She could kill the Delgado brothers.

"For the longest time," Dean said, "I thought it was coincidence, him becoming a spook like me. Then I con-nected the dots back to you." His voice was full of ac-cusation.

"I didn't do anything wrong." Yet, he stood here, wearing a mask and latex gloves, trying to make her feel as if she had. How dared he. "This isn't about me. This is about you. Remember? Take off that disguise and tell me why you need it. Right now."

Crossing her arms, she waited while he removed the mask. She wasn't going to back down until he spilled his guts. It was the very least that he owed her.

He looked up at her with his real face, and all her careful compartmentalization unraveled. Their days and nights together came back in a dizzying rush. Holding hands. Kissing. Sharing their highs and lows. Making love whenever they could, wherever they could, as often as possible.

Her heart pounded faster, her blood singing in her veins. She longed to press her palm to his cheek and caress his two-day stubble. Touch him. Verify with her hands, not only her eyes and her heart, that he was real. But she resisted the temptation.

The man was an itch she longed to scratch. But like a severe case of the chicken pox, if she indulged and gave in to the urge, it would only lead to scars she'd later regret.

"Why have you been lying to me for months, pretending to be DJ?" When he could have climbed a flight of stairs to her apartment, located right above the bar, and told her the truth. Given them a chance to talk, to heal.

A part of her desperately wanted to believe that he'd come back to town for her.

He lowered his head a moment, as if debating whether to be honest. So help her, she would shake it out of him if need be.

"I owe you the truth." His gaze met hers. "You can't repeat anything I tell you, not even under duress. When I chased after Smitty, my face was caught on CCTV.

People will come here looking for me. You've got to play dumb. For your sake. Do you understand?"

Without a doubt, she could play as dumb as she felt. For nine months she'd believed his charade, hook, line and sinker. Like a complete idiot.

"All right." She gestured for him to continue.

"I was with the CIA," he said, and the past tense struck her. "On my team's last mission, something went wrong. We—I—killed someone who was only supposed to die as collateral damage with the intended target. But the high-value target wasn't on-site. Everything went to hell in a handbasket. The CIA thinks that my team was turned, that we're traitors."

"What?" This was serious. Big. As in treason and jail time–type trouble.

She looked at him, really looked at him. This time she noticed the changes. He was older. More ridiculously attractive as a man than he'd been as a boy. But there was an intensity to him, a dangerous aura that hadn't been there when he was younger.

"My entire team was forced to scatter to the four winds and stay off the agency's radar."

"You need a lawyer. A real shark who swims in intelligence agency waters. The best money can buy." Too bad she didn't have two nickels to rub together.

"A lawyer?" he scoffed. "They don't want to arrest us and put us on trial. They want us dead. Permanently silenced. Erased from existence."

He was so steady and sure, the exact opposite of her. It made her doubt reality, but she shook her head. What he alleged was preposterous.

"You're an American citizen entitled to due process,"

she said. "What you're talking about only happens in movies. Not real life."

He moved into her space and pressed so close that the smell of him engulfed her senses. On reflex, her body tightened, guarding against it.

"Oh, Kate." He tucked a lock of her hair behind her ear, trailed his fingers along her jaw.

Heat jolted through her. His proximity, the warmth radiating from his body played havoc on her ability to think, to breathe.

The bone-deep ache she'd found hard to ignore for the last decade flared up as she stared at him. His luscious curls were long enough at the front to run her fingers through them. Skin she wanted to touch. Brown eyes that went straight through her.

She realized all the anger and sorrow and confusion she'd had festering inside would never end.

His presence, the memory of him, was an albatross around her neck.

"After I ran into you at the bar and realized you lived upstairs, every single day I thought about knocking on your door and telling you." His voice was soft as cotton. "Showing you who I really was. But this," he said, gesturing toward her, and the insult in his tone was clear, "is the reason I didn't."

Her stomach twisted into a knot. *"This?"*

"You're a candy-coated civilian ill equipped to handle the truth. I told you that my life is in danger, and you're in denial. Talking about lawyers and due process. I kill people for the CIA. Or used to. Bad people to make the world a better, safer place. Nonetheless, *assassin* would be the job title on my résumé. You wouldn't believe the things I've seen. The things I've done. That's how I know, for a fact, that a team will have boots on the ground in Laramie in twenty-four hours. Thirty-six, tops. They will have one objective—to eliminate me. So I'm going to be long gone by then."

Every word that left his mouth gathered momentum, building speed, barreling forward, and plowed into her with the force of an eighteen-wheeler.

It was a wonder she was still standing without shattered bones. But it was her heart that was in pieces. "I just found out that you're here and you're leaving tomorrow?"

She'd thought she had died inside when he'd disappeared the first time.

Stripped to nothing.

But now hurt was like a concrete block in her chest, weighing her down, making it impossible to breathe. How could he keep killing her?

"Not tomorrow," he said. "I'm leaving tonight."

Chapter Four

Ten minutes to talk to Kate was taking twenty. Dean needed to go.

The clock ticking in his head was counting down to the arrival of a very real team of trained killers, despite her doubts.

She squeezed her eyes shut as if in pain, her lips pinched. Her long hair fell forward, covering her face. Wavy and thick, it was still the color of sunshine. He remembered the silken feel of it between his fingers the same way he remembered the feel of her pressed against him. How she smelled of wild summer flowers even in winter.

In all his years, he'd never desired a woman the way he had her.

He pulled off his gloves, tucked her hair back and caressed her cheek. She was so beautiful, had the face of an angel. It tore him apart to see her upset.

"Kate?" He curled his hands around her arms, wanting to hold her, to make this better or at least easier, but he seemed to be making it worse.

She trembled in his hands, and it frightened him. All he wanted was to keep her safe and out of harm's way.

"Are you all right?" For the second time she didn't

respond. So he did the only thing he could think of. The one thing he'd longed to do the moment he'd set eyes on her again.

He lowered his mouth to hers and kissed her. His lips trembled, or maybe it was hers. For a heartbeat it was perfection. She stopped shaking, her body softening as she deepened the kiss. His bare hand cupped her face, her lips warm and soft under his.

And then that perfection disintegrated.

Wrenching back, she stumbled away from him, her eyes snapping open. She fixed him with a stare and wiped the back of her hand across her mouth as though he'd tasted rancid. "Why are you here in Laramie?"

The question caught him off guard, a complete blindside. "I don't understand."

"You're a superspy 007 knockoff now. You claim you're on the run and need to hide, so why come back home? Why did you pick Laramie?"

He shook his head. The answer was complicated. Convoluted on too many levels to explain in a hospital bathroom. Leaving all those years ago hadn't really been a choice. A terrible, necessary act to prevent something more horrible from happening. Every important thread in his life began and led right back here in a vicious tangle. Knotted up forever.

The one thread that shone the brightest was standing right in front of him—Kate.

But he chose one word to sum it all up. "Closure."

She pulled away from him with an anguished look on her face, as though he'd said the worst possible thing. "You're still the same selfish coward who ran away with his tail tucked between his legs fifteen years ago."

The accusation knocked the breath from his lungs.

His hands dropped from her arms, and he stepped back. "I'm a lot of things, but a selfish coward isn't one of them." He had risked his life countless times in the marines and with the CIA for his country and national security. To preserve a way of life he didn't have the privilege to enjoy.

"Is that what you tell yourself so you can sleep at night?"

He deserved her anger considering the way he'd handled things, but after all this time, he had assumed she would've guessed the reason he left. "Things had gotten bad at home."

"I know. I was there. I saw the bruises on you and Lucas."

But she'd only been aware of a fraction of the darkness he'd lived with. There had been so many things he'd been unable to say at the time. Even now.

Perhaps that's why he'd made a great bartender. He'd spoken little and had listened a lot, especially to her, over the past few months. That was his one other undervalued talent. Listening.

People loved to talk to him. Bartending was an easy cover. After he'd learned that Kate lived in the apartment above the bar, it had sealed his conviction to wheedle his way into the job.

Kate had been his anchor back then, and when his world had turned upside down again, fleeing for his life, he'd been drawn back here. To her.

"You don't know," he said, shaking his head.

"It takes courage to stay and fight for what you love. But that's not what you did, is it?" She took off his jacket and threw it at him. "You ran. Without saying goodbye.

If you need to go again, then do what you do best, and leave. But I could really use your help."

Hollow dread opened in his chest—a sinkhole threatening to swallow his future. "My help with what?"

"Figuring out what happened to Cheryl and making sure her baby is safe. I'm going to find out who she was, why she was scared and who sent her to me."

Dean sighed. "Let the sheriff handle it."

"The sheriff didn't see a pregnant, malnourished girl so terrified for her life and her baby's she went to a veterinarian instead of a hospital to give birth. As soon as Jim finds out that you, DJ, disappeared without a trace, he'll be more interested in your whereabouts than that infant."

"You're only going to invite trouble by asking questions." Dean got the sense that the situation with Smitty and his cohort had gone deeper than a lover's quarrel. If he had to guess, he would bet money this involved organized crime. They didn't have the mob out there in Wyoming, but they sure had shadowy figures doing dirty deeds. "Leave it alone."

"If I had looked the other way and left it alone, where would that baby be now?"

He shuddered to think of the possibilities. "Maybe one of them was the father and he was afraid she'd steal his kid. Maybe they only wanted the baby to use him as leverage with Cheryl because she saw or heard something she shouldn't have. Maybe with the three of them dead, there's nothing more to worry about." The list of maybes stacking up in his head seemed infinite.

"And *maybe* not. I'm going to dig until I get answers." Her tone brooked no argument.

"Why?"

"Because I'm not a coward. Because I think about

more than myself. Because I ushered that child into the world. In a way, he's my responsibility, since there's no one else to look out for him. And it's the right thing to do."

"But it's not the smart thing. You're only going to put yourself in danger."

"That's why I need you. Dean, if you hadn't been in the mobile clinic, those men would've killed me to get to her and the baby."

His gut roiled with renewed fury. He'd accepted the possibility of an early death a long time ago, but Kate was meant to live a long, happy life.

Her honey-brown eyes softened, drawing him in. "More thugs could turn up when I start asking questions. You're a slick agent with all sorts of useful skills. Who better to help me get answers while keeping me safe?"

The knot in the threads of his life tightened. But he couldn't get sucked into this.

"I can't stay." No matter how much he wanted to. He'd give anything for more time with her now that she knew who he was. "Pursuing this on your own could be suicide. Let it go, please. I don't want anything to happen to you."

"Then stay. For me."

Asking him to give her the Hope diamond would be simpler. Kate had no idea what was headed to Laramie. *Something deadly this way comes.* "I can't," he said.

She straightened, her eyes growing cold. "I thought about what it might be like to see you again one day. Good. Hard. Painful. But I hadn't imagined you'd be such a sad disappointment." She opened the bathroom door.

Dean caught her wrist and stopped her before she

crossed the threshold. "Give me a second to put this thing back on." He held up the mask. "Then I'll take you home."

He could talk some sense into her during the car ride, make her see reason.

"I don't need a ride. Child Protective Services is on the way. I'm going to hang around until they get here, so I have a point of contact. I'll get a car service to take me home when I'm ready to leave. Goodbye, Dean." The neutral finality in her voice stung.

Her wrist jerked free of his hand, and she was gone.

The door closed behind her.

He took a moment to gather himself and process what had transpired before pulling on his gloves and the mask. After making sure everything was in place with the bandanna covering his neck, he slipped into the hall.

Kate stood with her arms crossed over her chest, staring into the nursery.

He walked up beside her, his head down, staring at his boots.

This wasn't how he wanted to end things. The atmosphere between them was saturated with things unsaid. It didn't feel like closure. It felt like regret.

He noticed the outline of her cell phone in her lab coat pocket. He grabbed it and swiped the screen. The phone wasn't even password protected.

Candy-coated civilian.

In her contacts, he thumbed in the number to his burner phone—a prepaid disposable—not the fake number he'd given to the sheriff and saved it under the name Heathcliff. It was from her favorite book in high school, *Wuthering Heights*. He'd never understood why she'd loved it so much. The two lovers had married other people and died in the end without ever truly being to-gether. Then again, if suffering and tragedy were Kate's gold standard of a relationship, it explained why she'd fallen for him.

"If you need me, call." He held out the cell.

"I thought you were leaving with no plans to come back," she said without looking at him or taking the phone.

"I am."

"Then why bother giving me your number?"

"If you get into a jam or something—"

"You'll be halfway across the country. Maybe even in Canada. Mexico. You're a superspy. Not a superman."

She had a valid point. But he couldn't bear to think this would be the last conversation that they'd ever have.

"Take it anyway." He dropped the phone in her pocket, and it clinked against something that didn't sound like keys.

The sound drew both their gazes.

She stuck her hand in her pocket and pulled out a thumb drive. "Did you put this in there?" She finally met his eyes.

"No. I have no idea where that came from."

She flipped it over, examining the thumb drive. Silver and nondescript, there was nothing written on it. Kate's gaze roamed as though she was thinking. "Cheryl grabbed my pocket right before she died. I was still in shock from the fight and seeing you. She could have slipped this inside without my knowing."

"If that thumb drive came from Cheryl, whatever is on it will only get you killed."

Dean went to snatch the drive from her fingers, but

she clenched a fist around it and pulled it out of his reach. She was faster than he expected.

Raising an eyebrow, she asked, "Were you going to take this to help me?"

In a manner of speaking. "I was going to take it to save you." From herself.

"You don't care about me. And you don't care about him." She nodded toward the nursery.

Care about her?

For a while, he'd deluded himself into thinking that a person's first love was supposed to stick. That not being able to forget and move on didn't mean anything. Then he'd spent the past nine months seeing her, smelling her, talking to her and there was no denying that he was still *in love* with her. He'd never stopped caring. Had only suppressed his feelings over the years. Being back in Laramie brought it all to the surface.

But they weren't kids anymore. The stakes were higher.

This mess with Cheryl wasn't his problem, and it didn't need to be Kate's, either.

"You only care about yourself," she said, throwing another barb.

Guilt had gnawed at him for a decade and a half. To push his buttons, she was going to have to try a heck of a lot harder.

"Be smart and stay safe," he said. "Give the thumb drive to the sheriff."

"I'll give it to him after I make a copy of the contents."

Gritting his teeth in frustration, Dean shook his head. "Why won't you listen to me? Looking at what's on it will only drag you in deeper."

Kate shoved the thumb drive in the pocket of her

jeans. "I heard every word you said, but you're the one not paying attention. Cheryl chose me for a reason. I need to know why, and I need to make sure her son is going to be safe, too." She drew in a deep breath. "If something does happen to me," she said, her voice going cold, colder than outside, "and I mean the worst possible thing, do me a favor."

"What's that?"

"Don't come to my funeral. I wouldn't want you there." She turned away from him and faced the nursery. "This time stay gone for good."

His gut heated with that final blow from her, got so warm it turned something inside him to mush. Getting soft was the last thing he could afford with a team preparing to descend on this town. It was time to go. "My number is saved under Heathcliff," Dean muttered.

He walked to the elevator and hit the call button. In the shiny reflection of the doors, he watched her.

Her gaze stayed fixed on the nursery. Her bearing hard as granite.

The doors opened. He shuffled inside and looked at her one last time. His beautiful, stubborn Kate.

Not once did she glance in his direction.

The doors closed, and he wondered whether he was making a mistake.

Dean hurried out of the hospital, crossed the parking lot, hopped in his car and raced to the fleabag motel where he had a rented room. He had a long-term rate and an additional discount for taking care of his own upkeep. Convincing the manager that he was doing the motel a service by changing his own sheets, vacuuming and cleaning had been simple when in fact Dean would've paid extra to keep housekeeping from snooping through his belongings.

In his room, it took him two minutes flat to gather his things and pack. Traveling light was essential. He wiped down the surfaces as an extra precaution, taking special care in the bathroom.

He shoved a loaded nine-millimeter in his jacket pocket, took another quick look around to be sure he hadn't forgotten anything and left the room. Popping his trunk, he tossed his things inside. He peeled out of the motel parking lot, leaving his room unlocked, and got on the road. Within minutes, he hit I-80. The interstate was clear. It was nearly five in the morning.

Canada was a good idea. He could be in Calgary in less than sixteen hours.

But the farther the destination, the longer it would take him to get back when Kate called telling him she was in trouble. Not if, but when.

Taking the ramp for US Route 287 South, he headed toward Colorado. Denver was a great city, plenty to keep him occupied, but Boulder was a sounder choice with fewer surveillance cameras.

In the morning, he'd call his cousin Lourdes, though everyone called her Lola, and tell her to close up the bar. Take a vacation. Go back to Fort Collins. Her brother, Jake, was an FBI agent there. She would be out of danger with him in case the kill team showed up at Delgado's Bar.

Then there was Kate. When the time came, he could be back in Laramie in two hours from Boulder. And the time would come if she started asking questions about Cheryl. In his gut, he was certain of it.

Although the baby was safe, Child Protective Services was going to get involved and the sheriff's office would investigate, Kate wasn't going to leave well enough alone.

Not that it should surprise him. She'd always been like that. A backbone of steel, an iron will and the biggest heart. Even as a child, she couldn't resist picking up strays, nursing wounded animals and helping anyone in need.

In the sixth grade, they'd come across a lost dog on their way home from school. A vicious, mangy mutt with no collar. Dean had wanted to steer clear of the animal, suspecting that it might have rabies and one of them could lose a limb or an eye if they got too close.

All Kate had seen was a scared animal in need. Not taking heed of his warnings, ignoring the bared teeth and foaming drool dripping from its mouth, she'd followed her instincts and approached the dog. Dean had made Lucas stay back and climb on the hood of a nearby car just in case. The mutt had attacked and bitten her hand. Dean had grabbed her, pulling her up onto the car hood, but the dog managed to claw her leg in the process. Gave her scars that'd never fade.

Dr. Fitzsimmons, the local veterinarian, had been passing by, and he'd known exactly what to do to calm the animal and to treat Kate's wounds later.

Turned out, they'd both been right. The dog had been dangerous, but it hadn't had rabies. The mutt had been scared and mistreated.

Kate's instincts invariably got her into her trouble, at times badly hurt, but she was never wrong. Whatever she discovered on the thumb drive was only going to spur her on, not make her back off. Her heart had once been his compass, pointing him true north so that he didn't get lost. Digging into Cheryl might not be the smart thing, but Kate believed it was the right one. She also sensed that child was in danger.

Maybe he *was* the one not paying attention.

Kate thought what he did best was leaving, but the reality was, what he did best was protect her. Despite any pain it caused him.

Only a fool wouldn't be afraid of a kill team, but a marine's core tenet was to defend those who could not defend themselves. No matter the personal cost. Maybe Cheryl's child did need protection. Maybe not. There was only one way to know for sure. And if something happened to Kate because he didn't help her, because he was running like a selfish coward, albeit a smart one, what would his life be worth?

Dean crossed the border into Colorado, took the next exit and turned around, heading back to Laramie.

Chapter Five

"Thank you, Mrs. Smith, for coming in so quickly, at the crack of dawn, no less," Kate said to the representative from Child Protective Services.

"Once a call comes into the twenty-four-hour hotline, our office receives an email about the incident." Dressed in a pantsuit, Regina Smith was a middle-aged woman with glasses, a slight paunch and graying hair in a blunt bob that suited her round face. "I suffer from insomnia, and I'm constantly on the computer. A bad habit, I know. But it's fortunate I came when I did so I could get your account on what happened firsthand."

"All the information you provided was helpful. I feel better knowing you'll personally check on him once a day. I will as well, and the nurses promised to keep a special eye on him."

"I can speak with hospital security if you'd like. Have them do extra rounds on the maternity ward."

"That would be wonderful." Kate hadn't considered that possibility. "Are you sure they'll agree to do it?"

"The head of security and I are old friends," Mrs. Smith said with a smug grin.

Not surprising. There were only two degrees of separation from everyone in town.

"Hopefully the sheriff will be able to locate the deceased mother's family," Mrs. Smith said. "That would be the best-case scenario, placing the child with relatives. But either way, we'll ensure he's in a loving, stable home once he's cleared to leave the hospital." The older woman looked Kate over. "You should go home. Take a shower. Put on fresh clothes. Try to get some rest."

Kate glanced down at the bloodstains on her lab coat. She must've looked a hot mess. "Now that I've spoken with you, I'll call a car service."

"I can give you a ride, if you like."

"Are you sure? I don't want to put you to any trouble."

Flashing a warm smile, Mrs. Smith waved a dismissive hand. "It's no bother. After I drop you off, I'll grab a coffee and go in early to the office. Get started on the paperwork for Baby Doe."

"Thank you. I appreciate it."

They made their way down to the lobby and outside. The Arctic wind blowing down from the north cut straight through Kate. She tugged her lab coat closed and wrapped her arms around herself, fighting off a shiver.

Darkness still hung in the air. Wisps of gray clouds snaked around the moon high in the sky. The sun wouldn't be up for another hour or two.

Mrs. Smith pressed her key fob. Lights flashed on a late-model sedan as the doors unlocked. They both climbed in, and Kate gave a sigh of relief for the shelter from the cold.

"Where do you live?"

"In an apartment above Delgado's Bar."

"Oh, over on Third Street. You're right in the heart of town." Mrs. Smith headed out of the parking lot and turned onto Grand Avenue. "I've always wondered what those apartments were like. Are they nice?"

Kate shrugged. "Comfortable enough for the price. I get a hefty discount because mine is over the bar. It wasn't my first choice, but after…" She swallowed the words, not wanting to rehash the past.

"After what happened with Tyler," Mrs. Smith said with a shake of her head, finishing Kate's sentence, "you probably just wanted to get resettled anywhere quickly. You poor thing."

Kate cringed on the inside. Gossip spread through the small town like a communicable disease, but Tyler's death had made the front page of the newspaper. While out on one of his morning jogs, he'd been the victim of a hit-and-run driver. Killed instantly, according to the coroner. No witnesses. No suspects. His funeral had been a county event.

It'd been common knowledge she and Tyler had been involved and living together at the time.

"How did you know him?" Kate remembered Mrs. Smith from the funeral, but most of the town had shown up to pay their respects.

"His mom and I are good friends."

With all the friends and family relations, it felt like there was no separation in town. Not even two degrees.

Mrs. Smith tsked. "It's awful what happened. He was so young. Only thirty-three. His mother was hoping that Tyler would propose to you. She thought you would've made a fine daughter-in-law. A good wife."

Too bad Tyler wouldn't have made a good husband. Sure, he'd had a stable job, had been smart and funny and charming. Checked most of the appropriate boxes on the list for a suitable partner. But the dark secret she'd only shared with DJ—or rather, Dean—was that Tyler had been cheating on her. For months, she had suspected an affair. When she finally found proof that he'd been sleeping with his editor, she hadn't been angry or sad or humiliated.

Truth be told, she'd been relieved.

Tyler had given her a way out of a seemingly perfect relationship that half of Laramie had sworn would culminate in marriage.

Before Tyler's car accident, she had already made plans to move and had started looking for a new place. Then he'd died, and everyone had expected her to play the part of the bereaved girlfriend.

At the end of every relationship, she'd felt immense relief. A weight lifted from her.

Whether it had been future deputy sheriff Holden, the teller at the bank, the assistant professor at the community college or investigative journalist Tyler.

The only one she wished hadn't ended had been with the one guy who had broken her heart.

What did make her flush with the heat of humiliation was how she'd confided the truth to her bartender, not knowing she'd been pouring her soul out to Dean the whole time.

Mrs. Smith pulled up alongside the mobile pet clinic and stopped. "I'm so sorry for your loss. You and Tyler made such an attractive couple."

It had been ten and a half months, nearly a year, and still she received comments such as this, when to Kate it already felt like forever. "Thank you."

"I'll give my friend at the hospital a ring as soon as I think he's in the office."

Kate nodded. "I appreciate the ride." She hopped out of the car and waved goodbye as Mrs. Smith drove off.

She glanced at the mobile clinic. It would need a thorough cleaning. Not that she was sure if that was allowed. Was the truck considered a crime scene? She'd have to check with the sheriff and cancel her appointments for the day, perhaps for the next several if she didn't get the green light to sanitize it.

The EMTs had taken Cheryl's body and the baby so quickly. Kate tried to remember if she'd locked the truck. There was no cash in the clinic, but she had valuable equipment inside that someone could hock. A junkie had tried to break in once while she'd been living with Tyler.

One thing she loved about living over the bar was being able to keep an eye on the truck from her apartment.

She hurried up to the door. Sure enough, it was unlocked. *Fantastic.* Stepping inside, she hoped that nothing was missing. After the morning she'd had so far, she didn't think she could handle one more thing.

Kate climbed the three steps and stumbled to a halt. *Oh, my God!*

Things had been thrown and knocked around in the fight earlier, but now her truck had been completely ransacked. Her mind raced, choppy thoughts firing through her head as if in time with her pulse.

Someone had torn her clinic apart. Destroyed it.

Everything could be replaced, she told herself. Her insurance would cover the cost. It would be all right.

She stepped deeper inside. Medical instruments were scattered on the floor. The orthopedic saw, forceps, steel suture wire, stethoscope, handheld ultrasound. Equipment worth thousands of dollars hadn't been taken. She checked the locked medicine cabinet. It hadn't been touched.

This was so odd. Why would someone do this and not take anything?

Even as she drew in a deep, calming breath, telling herself this was a coincidence, it was as though a clammy finger ran down her spine.

What if Smitty had friends who wanted to send her a message? Had more than two men been looking for Cheryl? There must've been, if this was connected.

She eased back out of the truck, trying to come to grips with the vandalism. Part of her didn't think she was capable of handling this on top of everything else. What might happen when she started asking questions about Cheryl?

Backing down wasn't her style. She wasn't going to let some thugs intimidate her.

Closing and locking the door, she decided to take this one step at a time. First, coffee. Caffeine was a top priority. She needed to think clearly. After a piping-hot cup of joe, she'd call the sheriff's office and report the incident.

Kate slogged up the staircase to her place, vowing never to make the mistake of leaving home without her coat again. She pulled her keys from her pocket and unlocked the door. At least with the unexpected break from work, she'd be able to spend as much time as she wanted at the hospital and looking into Cheryl. Kate wasn't going to let this go. Something inside her wouldn't allow her to.

She crossed the threshold into the dim apartment, flinging the door shut. Warmth wrapped around her. She tossed her keys on the side table, switched on a lamp and headed for the kitchen.

A floorboard creaked behind her.

Kate froze as her blood ran cold. Someone was in her apartment. Then she heard it again, a soft groan of wood. She whirled around, facing the intruder.

A man wearing a ski mask stepped out of the shadows in the corner and into the faint light filtering in from the living room window. "Give me the thumb drive Cheryl stole." His voice was a harsh whisper.

For a split second, she couldn't move. Couldn't breathe. Then he took another step toward her, and adrenaline kicked in. Kate darted into the bedroom, slammed the door and twisted the latch on the knob, locking it.

The man banged against the door, making it rattle on its hinges.

She heard cursing from the other side. Frantically, she glanced around. She snatched her purse from the top of her dresser and dug inside.

Another loud bang against the door.

Oh, God, what's happening?

She grabbed the pepper spray for bears and thumbed off the orange safety guard as the bedroom door burst open. Shrieking, she aimed at the man's head and depressed the handle on the power fogger. A blast of pepper spray hit him in the face.

The guy reared back, roaring in pain.

If the spray could stop a bear with temporary loss of sight, burning the skin and restricting breathing, it'd certainly slow down a man.

She dashed into the bathroom and locked the door. Her mind reeled.

He's after the thumb drive. What's on it? Did he trash my truck looking for it?

She crossed the room and clawed at the latch on the frosted window. It had been painted over and was stuck. She took the metal nail file with a sharp pointed tip from the counter and scraped at the dried paint until the latch moved.

A faint popping sound drew her gaze. Bullet holes in the wood.

He had a gun. With a silencer.

She yanked the window up and climbed outside onto the fire escape. The door flew open, splintering around the frame, and the man stormed in.

Rubbing at his eyes and coughing, he waved the gun around wildly in his other hand and pulled the trigger. Bullets hammered into the walls.

Kate pinched her lips tight and climbed down the metal ladder.

Ping. Ping. Bullets ricocheted off steel near her head. In the quiet open air, the sound was loud and sharp. Almost earsplitting. She let loose a scream.

He was shooting at her.

More gunfire spit around her with sparks flying from the fire escape. She shrieked as she jumped from the last rung and hit the pavement. Pain zipped up her legs, and her heart slammed against her rib cage.

Move!

Run!

She scurried to her feet, ignoring the sharp ache in her ankles, and forced herself to think. Her mobile pet clinic was around the bend. But she remembered with a sinking heart that her keys were up in her apartment.

Footfalls pounded on the fire escape on the second floor. He was coming after her. She had to get out of there. Find help.

She scrambled to the corner and froze, thinking which way to go.

A car screeched to a halt in front of her. Hysteria bubbled up in her chest. *Oh, no.* Was it more of them?

Then she recognized the vehicle. A Jeep Renegade. Dean was behind the wheel. He leaned over and opened the passenger door. "Get in!"

A bullet struck the side mirror.

She lunged into the car and slammed the door shut.

Dean hit the accelerator, speeding away down the block.

Quivering, she slid down in the seat and wrapped her arms around herself.

"Are you okay? Did you get hit?"

He tried to kill me. He tried to kill me. He tried to kill me.

"Kate," Dean said, his voice growing firm, "were you shot? Are you okay?"

She couldn't speak. She just panted and shook her head.

"No, what?" he asked.

"I wasn't shot," she said, forcing the words from her mouth, but her voice was barely audible. She cleared her throat and tried again. "He didn't shoot me." But she was far from all right.

Dean made lots of dizzying turns, checking his rear-view mirror every block or two. Before she knew it, he parked in front of a motel on the outskirts of town. "I can't go back to the one I was staying at since the sheriff might go looking for me. I'll get a room here. We'll talk inside." He took her hand in his, and she wished he wasn't wearing gloves. "It's going to be okay."

A moment later his hand slipped from hers and he was

out of the car, moving toward the entrance. She thought about everything that happened in the past few hours to toss her world upside down.

All of it had started with a phone call for help. And landed her here. Outside a dump of a motel, running for her life.

Her chest convulsed as she pictured the man in the ski mask stalking toward her in her apartment. In her home. The one place that should've been safe.

A knock on the window startled her, making her jump. With a hand pressed to her chest, she tried to calm her racing heart.

Dean gestured for her to get out of the car, and she did.

"Here, the coffee is fresh." He handed her a to-go cup with a lid, steam escaping from the hole, and put his jacket around her shoulders. "We'll walk to the room. I'll repark away from the motel once I get you settled, just in case the sheriff puts out an all-points bulletin with the make and model."

He grabbed a bag from the trunk, put an arm around her, guided her to room 114 and unlocked the door. Inside it smelled of cigarette smoke and mildew.

She gazed at the faded green bedspread and sighed. In a handful of hours, this was what her life had become.

Dean locked the door and turned the heat up before urging her deeper inside the room, away from the door. He directed her toward the bed. She stiffened and pulled back, still too shaken, too terrified, but he was having none of it.

"It's okay," he reassured her and guided her to take a seat on the bed.

He sat beside her, so close that their legs and arms touched. His body was rigid, as if he were still on high alert, ready to handle any danger. He just sat there for a long moment, not saying anything, lending her his heat and the comfort of his nearness. Those dark eyes sharp on her face.

"You should drink the coffee." His tone was gentle. "Hope you still take it with two sugars and a splash of cream."

"I do. I'm surprised you remember something so inconsequential about me after all this time."

He pulled off the mask and removed the gloves. Caught her gaze and held it. "I remember everything about you."

A ghost of warmth flickered inside her.

"Go on and have some." He nudged the hand holding the cup up toward her mouth. "The sugar and a shot of caffeine will help counteract shock. I promise."

Taking an obedient sip of the coffee, she was glad to have something hot to drink and for Dean's presence. After she took another swallow, she actually felt a slight lessening of tension in his muscles, as though his worry was draining.

She lifted her head, suddenly more alert, her thoughts solidifying. "What are you doing here?" Not that she wasn't grateful to see him. If not for his fortuitous arrival, surely the man who'd broken into her apartment would've caught up with her. Dean had saved her for a second time. "I thought you'd left town."

"I did, but I couldn't stop thinking about you. How when it comes to you, no good deed goes unpunished. I'd never forgive myself if anything happened to you because I refused to help."

"You made it painfully clear that you weren't in a position to stick around."

"I'm not." He glanced at the clock on the nightstand. "It'll take a team time to mobilize. I figure I have a solid twenty to thirty hours before I need to worry." He put on a brave face, even managed a sad smile.

She envied his courage, wished she could fake it until it was real herself. "What happens at the thirty-hour mark?"

"I'll cross that bridge when I get to it."

Although she had asked him to stay, damn near demanded it, she didn't want him in any danger. To know that he was alive brought her soul-deep comfort. But she needed him. Now more than ever. As selfish and greedy as it was, she couldn't let him go. Not yet.

She latched onto the only hope she had. "If you hadn't come back…" Fear had a cold grip on her heart and tightened its grasp.

Shifting toward her, he rubbed her leg in slow, soothing strokes. "Tell me what happened at your apartment."

Kate brushed her hair out of her eyes with a trembling hand and took a deep breath, recalling the details. "I got a lift from the social worker. I remembered that I hadn't locked the clinic." A shudder rippled through her body, making the cup shake in her hand. "I was worried someone, a junkie maybe, might steal something. Inside, the truck had been trashed, but nothing valuable had been stolen. At first, I couldn't understand why anyone would deliberately vandalize the clinic. I went up to my place, and after I closed the door," she said, sucking in a sharp, shaky breath, "I realized that someone was in the apartment. I locked the bedroom door. But he busted in. I got him in the face with bear spray. Then I ran to the bathroom. Climbed out the window. And he started shooting at me."

A small, startling sound cut through the room, and she realized it had come from her. She clamped a hand over her mouth.

Dean brought her into his arms and wrapped her in a tight embrace. The dark tide of events was about to pull her under, drown her in the bleakness of it, but here in Dean's arms, it was as if he'd hauled her from the treacherous water into a life raft and towed her to safety. She doubted there would ever come a time when she didn't have feelings for this man.

She couldn't stop herself from leaning into his strength, his warmth. He held her, solid and steady, and it felt so good not to be alone. To be in his arms, to have him watching out for her, the way it used to be. Even if it was only for a few minutes and not permanent. Even though he was no longer hers.

He stroked her hair until the shivers stopped, cupped her chin and met her gaze. "It's okay." His husky voice soothed her, calming her frayed nerves. "You're safe now."

She swallowed, eye to eye with him as she nodded.

He shifted, taking her face between both hands. "I won't let anyone hurt you." His voice was soft and his breath was warm on her face.

He leaned into her, or she leaned into him. His lips brushed over hers in a gentle caress she welcomed. Testing. Tasting. So soft and sweet she wondered if she'd shatter from the shock of the sensation that light touch brought. Opening her mouth to let his tongue slide over hers, she kissed him back. A deeper, harder, long-awaited kiss that had her falling to pieces. He made a low, tortured noise in his throat like that of a wounded animal.

This is Dean. My Dean.

Relief seeped in every cell of her body. She had wanted this for so long, and it was so much better than she'd ever imagined.

He eased back, breaking the spell. His breathing was as shallow as hers, but there was regret in his eyes.

"I'm sorry," he said, rising to his feet.

I'm not.

"I didn't mean to take advantage again."

Again?

He meant in the hospital, when their wires had gotten crossed and his timing had been horrible. Who wanted to be kissed after he dropped the bombshell that he was packing up and skipping town, leaving her alone to re- solve the situation?

"You didn't take advantage. Dean—"

"Did you get a good look at him? The guy who broke in."

She shook her head, not wanting to think about that. Not when she could be kissing Dean. "No, he wore a ski mask."

"Did he say anything? Tell you what he wanted?"

"Yes. He wanted the thumb drive that Cheryl had taken."

A grim expression replaced the one of concern on his face, and she could practically hear his thoughts. *I told you so.*

Her jaw clenched hard, because he was right. She hated that he was right.

But he was too kind to gloat. That was one of the many things she'd loved about him. She was glad that hadn't changed.

"Do you still have the drive?" he asked.

"Of course." She dug in her pocket and pulled it out.

"The guy who broke into your apartment believes you have it. At this point, I think the only way out for you is forward. We have to take a look and see what kind of trouble Cheryl dragged you into."

Chapter Six

The dawn felt shredded as the sun began to rise. It was an eerie yellow, ringed with red. The color of an infected wound.

A bad omen.

Dean missed his team. *Topaz*. With Hunter Wright, Zenobia "Zee" Hanley and Gage Graham at his side, they'd get to the bottom of this in no time, eliminating any threats to Kate and the baby, making the world a safer place. That's what they did. Or rather, used to.

But he was on his own this time. No support. No backup. No computer whiz to work her digital magic.

Drawing the curtains in the room, Dean would've given anything to get Kate back in the car and head straight out of town, but that wasn't an option.

He pulled his laptop from his bag and plopped down beside her. After firing it up, he slipped the thumb drive into the USB port, hoping it was encrypted. No one would expect Kate, a local veterinarian, to crack that level of security. Under those circumstances, once she turned it over to the sheriff and it became public knowledge the drive was no longer in her possession, she wouldn't be in any danger.

Dragging the mouse onto the folder, he tapped the icon. It opened. There was no encryption.

His heart sank. The hope of an easy out for Kate deflated like a balloon. She was stuck in this mess.

The folder contained a series of Excel spreadsheets. Dated by month and year. He tapped on the most recent one.

The first column was a series of coordinates, degrees, minutes and seconds. Ten of them. Beside those were dates and times.

"This must be some kind of a schedule," he said.

"For what?"

"I don't know. Something illegal for sure."

Next to the dates was a list of numbers, ranging from one to two digits. The last column was money.

A lot of money.

"What is all this?" Kate asked.

Dean opened a couple of the other spreadsheets. More of the same, but the numbers in the last two columns varied. The coordinates didn't change. "Maybe it's drug-related," he said, thinking out loud. "If this column—" he pointed to the second to last with one- to two-digit numbers "—is for weight of product, say, in kilos, then the staggering amount of money would make sense."

She shot him a skeptical glance. "A major drug operation here?"

Why not? "You said yourself you had been worried about a junkie breaking into the clinic."

"I know," she said with a slight shake of her head, "but I guess I hadn't considered the bigger implications of it."

"There are drugs and addicts willing to buy everywhere. You just need to know where to look." That gave him an idea he hoped he wouldn't regret pursuing. "I should go to one of these locations and check it out. It's the only way to know what's going on."

"No, don't." Another shake of her head, more forceful, her face tense with worry. "It might be dangerous."

No *might* about it. "We need to know what Cheryl was involved in. What you're now in. That man who was in your apartment might come back."

She reeled back, staring at him. "I'll turn the thumb drive over to the sheriff."

"That'll prove you had it in the first place. You'll be a loose end someone might want to tie up. Or once the sheriff investigates, you could be a target of retribution for turning it over."

With her shoulders slumping, she reached across him to set her coffee on the nightstand next to the laptop. She propped her elbows on her knees and dropped her head into her hands.

He hated highlighting the worst possibilities for her, but she needed to know. It was the only way to make a decision. The more information, the better.

Dean put a palm to her back and felt a shudder run through her. His fingers tingled with the urge to glide through her thick hair and rub the nape of her neck.

Which was the wrong impulse, since he wouldn't be able to stop there. Then he'd want to hold her, kiss her again…

His attraction to her was still visceral, a craving he longed to satisfy.

Why did the wrong impulses have to feel so right?

"Oh, Dean," she said on a sigh.

He did everything he could to ignore the tightening in his body as a result of the way she'd uttered his name mingled with that soft sound. For too many nights the memory of *that*—the two of them as close as a man and a woman could be, physically, emotionally, that sound rolling from her lips—had been torture.

On other nights, it had been the only thing to get him through.

"We'll get to the bottom of whatever this is, find a way for you to be safe. I won't leave until we do."

"But what about the kill team?"

Nothing was ever simple. Was it? "Sitting around waiting for them to arrive is suicide. Pretty much like you handling this on your own." If he had to choose between her and himself, well, there was no choice at all. He would lay down his life for hers, any day, any time. Without hesitation.

Kate cringed as her face wrenched in worry. "It wasn't fair of me to ask you to help." Tears glistened in her eyes. "I'm sorry. It was selfish."

This was an impossible position. "You're concerned about a motherless newborn. That's the opposite of selfish. I'm glad I came back. You needed me." *Still do.*

"It's such a big risk for you to take."

She was worth it.

"I've got some time before that team will get here." If he was lucky. "I can do a lot of digging in twenty-four hours." But he'd stay longer to ensure she was safe.

"There's so much to figure out, and we haven't even had a chance to talk. That's not much time."

No, it wasn't. No time at all when he wanted weeks with her. Months. Years. A lifetime. "I'll make it work."

He put an arm back around her, bringing her close, and held her. He understood her distress and only wanted to alleviate it.

She rested her head in the crook of his neck. With his

other hand, he caressed her face, running his thumb across her cheek. Her skin was delicate under his fingertips.

Everything inside him warned he should drop his hand, but he held her tighter instead, tracing her jawline with his thumb.

She clutched his leg, and he tensed. Shifting, she looked up at him, and her mouth was suddenly dangerously close to his.

Touching her, being touched by her—hell, sitting next to her on the bed and staring into those sad, gorgeous eyes—dredged up memories. Passionate, raw, painful. None he'd trade. Not of her.

But the past wasn't what he needed to focus on. Neither was the present, with the scent of her hair filling his nose or the softness of her skin still pressed to his palm. Or with his lips tingling to taste her again.

Finding answers and keeping her safe was the only thing he should be thinking about.

"I should go," he said, dropping his hands from her and standing. "This is a good time for me do some recon." Not ideal with the sun rising, but it was manageable. This early in the morning, there wouldn't be much security at the locations on the spreadsheets, and any present would be lackadaisical. More concerned about getting a cup of coffee and breakfast than worried about catching an intruder.

"Maybe I should come with you," she said.

Definitely not. "It's better if you stay here. I'll know you're safe and out of harm's way. This will be easier and faster if my focus isn't split. Just promise to sit tight and don't leave. Okay?"

"Sure. I'll wait for you. Where else am I going to go?"

"Try to rest while I'm gone."

She looked up at him with exhaustion and fear in her eyes. "Highly unlikely. I'll be worried sick about whether you're all right the entire time."

"You saw me handle myself against two of those thugs. Have a little faith." He tucked her hair behind her ear and cupped her face. Her skin was velvety perfection, with a milky complexion that would show the imprint of a hard kiss. He recalled marking her with his mouth years ago, kissing his way down her body until he reached the soft, sensitive folds between her legs. *God*, he needed to get out of that room. "You should still try to sleep. You haven't had much rest." He dropped his hand and turned to the computer.

"You haven't had any."

"I'm trained to go without it for a few days. I'll be fine." He looked over the coordinates and homed in on two on the list. One was in Laramie and the other near Rock River. No need to write down either. He had been trained to memorize things on the fly: telephone numbers, addresses, license plates. Coordinates. "I'll call you when I'm headed back. If you haven't heard from me in four hours, then it means something went wrong." He estimated it should take him no longer than two. Padding the time was only a precaution. Hiccups happened, and there was no need to worry her unnecessarily. He grabbed his keys and headed for the door. "In the meantime, get some sleep."

"Dean." She stared at him, and his heart squeezed at the look in her eyes. "Please be careful."

"I always am."

WARM AIR HIT Lucas Delgado as he strolled through the automatic doors into the lobby of CIA headquarters in

Langley. He glanced at the giant American flag hanging from the rafters of the atrium. The security officers at the turnstiles were watching, observing everything, as always. There wasn't much to see yet. Give it another hour and there would be a steady stream of folks passing through.

Lucas scanned his badge and entered his code, clearing the security checkpoint. At the bank of elevators, he hit the call button. He sipped his protein smoothie, and his muscles loosened with gratitude after his grueling one-hour workout. Every day he pushed himself hard, switching up the focus of his exercise, but he never took a rest day.

Rest was for the weary.

The elevator chimed, and the doors opened.

He stepped inside and hit the button for his floor. He'd be the first one there in his section. Two hours before everyone else normally arrived, with the exception of the directors, Andrew Clark, Kelly Russell and Wayne Price. Those three practically lived here.

Lucas was making a name for himself. A fast burner and rising quickly. The first one in, the last to leave, never griped about an assignment and did anything that was necessary to accomplish the mission. *Anything.* Endured broken ribs, had taken a couple of bullets. Accepted the fact that collateral damage was a part of the job.

His old supervisor had taken notice, given him glowing performance reports, told him to keep up the stellar work and promoted him. All his hard work and sacrificing a life for the sake of his career had finally paid off.

Now he was running with the big dogs as a member of Team Cinnabar.

The name sounded innocuous, even sweet. Like candy or a breakfast treat you could buy at the mall by the dozen.

It was actually a mineral that resembled quartz in its symmetry and optical characteristics, but looks could be deceiving. Although cinnabar was mesmerizing and beautiful, it was also the deadliest mineral known to man.

Lucas was right at home with his new team.

With a ding, the elevator doors opened.

His team leader, a formidable man with sharp features and a permanent scowl, was standing in the hall. Fierce, no-nonsense Butch Helms. "Good. You're in early."

"I'm always in early. What are you doing here at this hour?"

"Waiting for you." Butch gestured for him to get out of the elevator. "I tried your cell, but it was turned off."

"I was in the gym and came straight here," Lucas said simply, with no need to explain further.

Headquarters was a sprawling compound, not a single office building, where thousands worked. The parking lot was color-coded like it was at Disneyland. There was a gym on-site, but the protocol was the same for all the buildings—no cell phones allowed.

He hadn't bothered to check for messages while traveling between the gym and the main building.

Lucas strode into the hall, feeling a sudden rush of adrenaline with each step. "Why are you looking for me?" he asked, too quickly, too forcefully.

If the team had a priority mission, then Butch would be waiting for everyone to arrive in their section, the vault—a locked suite of cubicles and offices set behind a heavy vault door. The design was the same for every section.

"An off-the-books assignment from Clark."

The director of the Special Activities Center, responsible for covert and paramilitary operations.

"For the team?" Lucas asked, dumbfounded.

"No, for you." Butch started walking down the hall, and Lucas got in step beside him.

Of course it was for him. Otherwise this conversation would be happening in the vault with the entire team. Still, Lucas didn't understand. "Why me?"

Not that he wasn't grateful to be chosen. Any chance to shine he'd seize with both fists. But only an idiot wouldn't look a gift horse in the mouth in this place.

"I got a call an hour ago to come in. Clark wants you. But he needed to check with me first."

"To see if I was available?" But that could've been discussed over the phone. No need to haul him in two hours early.

"No, to make sure you were up for the challenge."

"When have I ever not been?" Lucas asked, letting his defensive tone mask his nerves. Why were his competence and capabilities being called into question? He might not have worked very long with Butch, but Lucas had a flawless record that spoke for itself.

"This is different."

"Different how?" Lucas didn't appreciate surprises. Not even as a child. He'd always hated them. In his experience, they were rarely good.

Butch turned the corner to the left. Clark's office was to the right. They were heading toward the offices of the higher-ups. The deputy director for operations and the director of the Central Intelligence Agency were at the end of this hall.

"You'll see," Butch said. "You better not disappoint."

On the right was Kelly Russell's office suite. The executive assistant wasn't in yet. The light was on in Russell's office with the door partially open, but she wasn't at her desk.

Once again they went to the left.

The director's assistant waved them through. "They're waiting for you. No need to knock."

Butch snatched the smoothie from Lucas's hand and set it on the assistant's desk before opening the door.

"Come in," Director Wayne Price said, seated at his large mahogany desk.

Andrew Clark was leaning back in one of the two chairs facing the director.

Kelly Russell, the ice queen, was standing beside Price at his right hand. With her arms crossed, cobalt-blue eyes hard as sapphires, red hair pinned up in a bun, wearing a perfectly tailored suit as though it were a coat of armor, she looked like a mighty archangel ready to smite someone. The woman emanated power.

Butch took the other seat, leaving Lucas to stand.

He assumed a firm stance, feet planted wide, hands behind his back. The military at-ease position was the most comfortable for him after his time with the marines.

"Do you know why you're in here?" Price asked Lucas.

"No, sir."

"Are you aware of what happened with Team Topaz?"

The shocking news had spread like wildfire, burning everyone's ears. "That's classified, sir."

Price exhaled sharply with a disgusted look. "Don't

waste our time by making us explain something you might have already heard. Do you know?"

This was one of those gray, sticky areas. Admitting you knew too much could invite suspicion and an investigation. Lucas didn't mind gray, but he steered clear of sticky.

"The teams have heard rumors," Butch said, like a good team leader protecting his own. "Nothing concrete. Nothing official. You know us, too busy with our noses to the grindstone."

And too damn smart to ask questions.

Price gestured to Clark.

"Topaz went rogue," Clark said. "They were paid to murder an Afghan official. A half a million each in offshore accounts. Then they disappeared."

Lucas's gaze slid to the ice queen, looking for a reaction. All he saw was a block of permafrost.

She had been Topaz's handler on that mission. To his knowledge, no one had investigated *her*.

After one of her teams went up flames, she'd been promoted. From handler to director of operations, effectively skipping Clark's position.

There were whispers about that, too. All behind her back. No one was dumb enough to say anything to her face. Everyone feared her.

Before the fiasco with Topaz, every team had vied to have her as their handler. She was the sharpest, the shrewdest strategic thinker and would cut down anyone who dared get in her way or that of her team.

Questions hung in the air. A stench everybody hoped would pass given enough time since it was clear they were grooming Russell to take over as director one day.

"Gage Graham and Zenobia Hanley popped up on

our radar," Clark continued. "In Virginia and Alaska, respectively. We sent cleanup teams after them."

Mercenaries who took care of the CIA's dirty work at a far enough distance to provide plausible deniability for the director.

Official teams, such as Cinnabar, and once upon a time Topaz, handled high-level on-the-books black ops missions.

"Both teams failed," Clark said.

"This time we're considering a different approach," Price said. "One Kelly recommended."

Glances shifted to her. Still, she said nothing.

"This time, sir?" Lucas asked.

Clark crossed his legs. "Around three this morning, we got a lead on your brother, Dean."

Surprised whipped through Lucas, making his heart skip a beat. He had guessed this conversation was going to end up on the topic of Dean, but hearing his name out loud and that he'd made a mistake, exposing his whereabouts, caught Lucas off guard. What Dean lacked as a brother he made up for tenfold as an operative.

"We may be blood and share a surname," Lucas explained, "but he's not family to me."

Price and Clark exchanged an inscrutable look. Russell's gaze stayed glued to Lucas.

"I trust this is no surprise to you," Lucas said. "Otherwise I suspect that I wouldn't be in your office." He had no allegiance to that traitor. His loyalty was to his country. To the agency. To his team. Since he started working there, he'd made certain that was common knowledge to everyone.

Price gave a curt nod.

"We want to send you after your brother, Dean," Clark

corrected. "Your assignment will be to find him. Then get close. Close enough for him to trust you. Get him to tell you where the others are hiding. We want the entire team. Dead. This problem needs to be buried."

Price propped his elbows on the arm of his chair and steepled his fingers in front of him. "You don't have to be the one to pull the trigger."

Lucas stiffened. There was no wave of relief. No great sense of disappointment. He felt nothing one way or the other about whether Dean lived or died. Or, for that matter, who killed him. What they were asking him to do wasn't a betrayal. He didn't owe Dean anything. In fact, it was the other way around.

But it unsettled him that they thought him incapable of pulling the trigger. That they wanted to give him an easy out. One he didn't want.

"You won't be alone," Clark said in a soothing tone, as though Lucas needed reassurance.

"Then this is a Team Cinnabar assignment," Lucas said to Clark while looking at Butch.

"No, no," Clark said quickly. "We can't send Cinnabar on this. There's already too much exposure for us by sending you. But if something goes wrong, it's easy enough to explain your involvement, considering your familial ties, on paper."

Lucas straightened. "You mean I'm disposable."

In the event the impossible happened and he didn't do his job and fled with Dean, they'd say it was in the blood, being a traitor. Bound to happen. Then there was the flip side, where he succeeded but things got complicated: too much collateral damage, law enforcement was drawn into the mix or, the worst for a covert operative, he was identified while operating illegally on American soil.

Either way, they could spin the story, claim he went rogue. Like Dean.

"More like viable. *Disposable* is such an ugly word," Clark said.

That didn't make it any less accurate.

"You're not a Lego block, easily replaced. We've invested a great deal of money in your training." Clark uncrossed his legs and shifted uncomfortably in his chair. "You provide—"

"Plausible deniability," Lucas said, finishing his sentence.

"Yes." Exhaling with visible relief, Clark nodded. Even gave a little grin. "That's the brilliance of Kelly's plan."

Lucas's gaze lifted, meeting her intensely blue eyes. Not a peep from her.

"I still have a concern," Price said, drawing Lucas's full attention once again, "despite assurances from Kelly and Butch."

"What's that, sir?"

"We're asking a great deal here. For you to turn on blood. I understand the two of you are estranged, but I'm finding it difficult to believe that when it comes down to it, you'll follow through."

Lucas drew in a long, steady breath while screaming on the inside. The last thing he should have to do was prove he had no *viable* relationship with Dean.

He had two options. One, he could spill his guts about why he already considered Dean dead as far as he was concerned. Open an old wound and bleed all over the floor, showing them his pain, resurrecting the anger.

Or he could take option number two. "My primary objective is to discover the whereabouts of Team Topaz, is that correct?"

"Yes," Price said. "That's right."

"After the primary objective is met, do I have permission to complete the secondary?"

Price leaned forward, brows drawing down, as he rested his forearms on the desk. "Are you seriously asking if you can kill your brother?"

They weren't biological brothers by choice. Not a damn thing Lucas could do about his DNA, and he shouldn't be punished or held back professionally because of it. "I'm asking if I have clearance to pull the trigger and eliminate a target. Dean Delgado is no different than any other. That man means nothing to me."

The day Dean left him behind, he'd made it crystal clear that Lucas had meant nothing to him, either.

"You're sure you're capable of looking Dean in the face and putting a slug in his head?" Price's eyes narrowed as he studied him.

The hard part would be playing nice with Dean and gaining his trust. Not killing him. "Absolutely."

"All right," Price said, appearing resigned. "But due to the precarious nature of this assignment, the kill team will be wired to hear *and* see everything you do."

Yes! The assignment was his.

"The team is being put together now," Clark said. "I'll send you the file with everything we have on Dean. Wheels up in ten hours out of Dulles. Flight time will be four."

"How exactly did he pop up on your radar?" Lucas asked, the question now occurring to him after the stress of securing the mission had passed.

"An analyst caught him on CCTV with facial recognition," Clark said. "In Laramie, Wyoming."

Lucas flinched before he caught himself.

Price narrowed his eyes again. "I understand it's your hometown. Is that going to be a problem?"

Lucas smiled. "On the contrary." That fool went back home. Because of *her*, and he didn't mean their mother. He didn't care about the woman who'd given birth to him. Heartless SOB. No, Dean had gone back for Kate. On the inside, Lucas rolled his eyes. He would bet dollars to doughnuts that he'd find Dean within sniffing distance of Kate Sawyer. "I think it'll be easier than I first anticipated."

Price nodded in approval.

"One last question," Lucas said. "If you pinpointed Gage Graham in Virginia and Zenobia Hanley in Alaska, what makes you think that Dean knows where the others are now?"

Team Topaz was comprised of the best operatives the CIA had. They were smart enough not to stay in contact with each other. Weren't they?

"We have reason to believe," Price said, giving Russell a flinty side glance, "that if the members are put under enough pressure, they'll reach out to their old team leader, Hunter Wright. A last measure sort of thing."

"We already put Graham and Hanley in a pressure cooker," Clark said. "You can do the same with Dean. Use the mercs we're sending with you. Play good cop, bad cop."

"But Hunter Wright is one of the best. Why would he give them a way to contact him? That would leave him exposed, vulnerable if they were captured."

"We have it on good authority," Clark said, his gaze

bouncing between Lucas and Russell, "that Hunter's one weakness is his team. Safeguarding them, even at risk to himself. Get to Dean and we can find the rest of them."

Lucas stared at Kelly Russell. She stood there, as if she were an innocent bystander with clean hands, a dutiful solider ready to smite upon the orders of Price. When in fact the ice queen was pulling the strings behind this entire operation. "You were their handler—"

Butch shushed him, like Lucas was a dog that had to be controlled.

And it worked well enough to give him pause, but if Lucas didn't finish now that he'd started, he'd lose respect, and rightfully so. "As I was saying, ma'am, you were their handler. You haven't said a word against Topaz or for them, to any of the teams." She could sit in that fancy new office of hers and move on with her life. Put this debacle behind her. But she wasn't. She was in Price's office, stirring the pot. "So why are you spearheading this?"

"Because Topaz needs to learn," Kelly Russell finally said, softly and slowly, her eyes narrowing until they were catlike, "that you don't bite the hand that feeds you. No one crosses me, betrays this country and this institution, spitting on every value we hold sacred, under my watch, and lives to brag about it."

All righty.

This was why everyone feared her. Probably Price, too.

"Yes, ma'am," Lucas said.

Clark cleared his throat, but it did little to clear the suffocating tension in the room. "I'll send the file over now. And Lucas, this is vital for us. Succeed and you'll write your own ticket in SAC," Clark said, referring to the Special Activities Center.

This time, Lucas smiled on the inside. Ambition was a ball of fire in his chest. If he had to incinerate Dean down to scorched earth to achieve his goals, so be it. Dean had brought this on himself, in more ways than one.

Butch stood.

That was their cue to leave.

"Thank you for this opportunity," Lucas said to the room before focusing on Russell. "Ma'am." She was the one who'd given it to him.

Lucas turned toward the door with Butch right on his heels.

"See, I was right about him," Russell said to Price and Clark, her tone smug.

"Never should've doubted you, Kelly," Price said as Lucas reached the threshold. "That kid is a real predator."

"I'm counting on it," Russell said.

Butch closed the door.

Lucas tipped his head in thanks to the assistant and grabbed his smoothie. This was precisely the kind of assignment he needed. He might not be on his own, but the team was only backup. This mission was his.

If he pulled it off—*no, not if*, when he pulled it off—the glory would be all his, too. No sharing the credit with anyone.

Once they cleared the office suite and reached the hall, Butch stopped him. "Hey, you were pretty convincing back there. The only reason you made it into that office in the first place is because the ice queen chose you and I vouched for you. Do you understand what I'm saying?"

If he screwed up, there would be hell to pay. This assignment would make or break his career. "I understand."

"I'm not sure you do. If you don't succeed, they'll question your loyalty to the agency. To the country. They'll wonder if you're a threat to national security like your brother."

One more reason for Lucas to hate Dean.

"Between you and me," Butch said, "I need the real answer. Once you get the information on the others in Topaz, can you kill him?"

In this life, there would be no forgiveness for Dean. They'd never get square, be good with one another. Not after what Lucas had had to endure alone. Maybe after Dean was dead. "Without a doubt, I can kill him."

"Good. I believe you. But remember that killing him isn't your primary objective. Finding Topaz is," Butch said. "You probably think you know Dean, but I caution you not to underestimate him."

Lucas wasn't kidding himself. He didn't know Dean any more than Dean knew Lucas. They were strangers with the same last name and a shared childhood. Nothing more.

Dean was a highly skilled operative, and Lucas wouldn't forget it.

"I won't."

"Good," Butch said. "Let's go talk about a contingency."

"Contingency for what?" Lucas asked.

"To cover you in case things don't go the way you plan. Expect the unexpected." Butch put a hand on his shoulder, his grip firm. "You're Cinnabar now. We don't fail."

Chapter Seven

Time was short. Dean needed to check out at least one location on the spreadsheet and decided to go with the one to the south of town. After plugging the coordinates into the satellite navigation system, it was only a fifteen-minute drive.

When the satnav pinged that he was a quarter mile from his destination, he knew precisely where he was headed. To an old, abandoned cement plant. The place was on the far outskirts of town and large enough to hide any illicit activity and not draw attention from law enforcement.

Almost at the plant, he drove close enough to park his car out of sight and approach on foot. He didn't bother with the synthetic mask. Instead, he pulled the stretchy fabric of the bandanna up to cover his mouth and nose. A knife and a gun with attached sound suppressor were both good choices to avoid drawing unwanted attention, but he also brought along zip ties and duct tape. Getting entangled in a one-on-one fight or taking on multiple guards would be a last resort. He'd prefer not to engage with anyone. An alarm could be sounded, a phone call could be made and the whole enterprise might close shop and relocate before the sheriff had an opportunity to investigate.

He left his Jeep and headed for the target.

No danger of pedestrian traffic out here. No residences for miles. Doing a full perimeter sweep around the building from a safe distance gave him a chance to choose his point of entry and determine whether it was under surveillance. He hadn't spotted any guards yet, but there were three vehicles parked around the side of the plant behind a brick wall, hiding them from view of any passersby from the road.

Old crates were stacked up in a maze between the vehicles and the building. He ducked in the shadows, observing and listening, as long as he dared before changing position. Moving at the right moment was as crucial as recognizing the difference between patience and paranoia. To slip in and out unnoticed, his timing had to be on point.

There was no suspicious activity on the outside of the plant and no sign of anyone coming to investigate as if aware of his presence. A security camera hung by a hinge above the door and was obviously not functional. A remnant of when the plant had been operational. This was as good as it was going to get.

He checked the doorknob, but it didn't turn. Locked. It took precious minutes to pick it quickly and quietly. Not his favorite activity. Gage was much better at this than he was, but the tumbler was a simple one, old and no longer secure.

Proper safety measures weren't high on the priority list of whoever was in charge of this operation. Then again, no one probably thought to come snooping around a defunct cement plant.

He proceeded inside, easing the door closed behind him, and immediately hugged one wall under the cover of a set of stairs. There were noises mixed with the faint murmuring of voices farther away. Not loud enough to pick up on what was being said, but he recognized the rhythm of conversation. It wasn't coming from the upper level, though. The sounds originated somewhere down on the ground floor.

Crouched low, he advanced into the plant and kept behind cover as much as possible. The air was musty and stale, heavy with dust. But that was to be expected in a place that had once manufactured cement.

Every time he changed position, slipping deeper into the facility, he took calculated glimpses of the plant and his surroundings, listening hard along the way. The more he exposed himself to see what was going on, the more likely someone would spot him. A delicate balance that he had to get right.

He swept closer to the center of the facility, toward the faint sounds of movement and chatter. Maybe three guys. No more than five. All probably armed. But he had no intentions of finding that out the hard way.

Ducking behind boxes and skirting in between old equipment, he inched even deeper.

The men were concentrated in an open area just ahead. Dean could tell by the increase in the volume of voices and how the sound carried with a bit of an echo. This was it. Right around the corner was the reason he'd come here.

He inched out from behind his cover and froze, his every muscle tensing.

A guard was standing less than a foot away with his back to Dean. The guy was tall, but lanky. Yawning, he stretched and scratched his shaggy hair that looked greasy and in need of a good washing.

Two hundred feet away were more men. Four, from what Dean could tell with the other guy blocking his view.

Tense and poised, he waited, ready for the opportune moment to strike. The other men were busy moving something, distracted with chitchat. Once all four had their line of sight shifted the other way, Dean leaped into action.

He crept up behind the guy. In one lightning-fast move, he threw an arm around the guy's throat. Neck locked in the crook of Dean's elbow, the man strained to break loose. Before he kicked something, making noise and drawing attention, Dean yanked him back behind a concrete pillar. He increased the pressure on the guy's throat, closing his windpipe, until the lack of oxygen made him lose consciousness. When the man went limp, Dean laid the guy down on the ground and reached into his back pocket, pulling out a few zip ties to bind him and some duct tape to cover his mouth.

Securing the guard and preventing him from alerting anyone to Dean's presence was better than killing him. After he came to, it would take him plenty of time to wriggle into sight and catch someone's attention. By then, Dean planned to be long gone. Once they eventually found their buddy restrained but alive, they shouldn't feel threatened enough to relocate whatever business they had going on, especially since no product had been stolen.

If anything, they'd increase and tighten security. But that was the sheriff's problem.

With a guard down, he needed to move more quickly.

Find out the nature of this operation and get the hell out of there. He glanced around the pillar.

There were two long tables set up. The guys were sorting little bags and boxing them up, but he couldn't make out what it was. He had to get closer for a better look.

Dean darted behind some equipment, a cluster of cone crushers—compression machines used to take in raw materials and reduce them in size. He peeked out in between two of the large machines.

They were weighing the resealable plastic bags on food scales and boxing them up. Inside each small baggie were clear, chunky crystals resembling ice.

Crystal methamphetamine.

In his gut, he'd known it was drugs. But had no idea which one.

Although the price of meth was comparable to that of cocaine, demand for methamphetamine was greater because it produced longer-lasting effects and was more readily available, thanks to the organized crime groups and people trying the cook the stuff in their garages.

His head was filled with all sorts of *not-so-fun* facts that were useless at a party with civilians as a part of his job.

This site was clearly a hub, a delivery and storage point, because they weren't cooking the stuff here.

So, what was going on at the other locations?

KATE FELT GUILTY for being exhausted and wanting to sleep, but her mind was spinning in circles and her paranoid thoughts no longer made any sense. To think straight, she had to rest. She curled up on the bed and pulled the blanket over her.

She replayed the incident in the mobile pet clinic. How

Dean must have sensed the threat since he had turned toward the door before it had been wrenched open. The way he had launched into battle mode, putting down a very large and scary Smitty and then taking on a second man. His reflexes had been sharp, fast as a hairpin trigger, and he was strong.

He'll be okay.

If anyone could take this on out there alone, it was Dean.

Bit by bit, she relaxed and gave in to the heaviness tugging at her eyelids. The darkness called to her, and she surrendered.

Her phone rang, and she jerked awake.

Dean!

What if he was in trouble?

She fumbled for her phone in the dark room and blindly answered it. "Dean, is everything okay?"

"Katie," Jim said on the other end of the line. "Are you all right?"

"Oh, uh…" Pulse spiking, she sat up in the bed and organized her thoughts. "Yes, I'm fine. What can I do for you?"

"We received a call from one of your neighbors. He reported gunshots and a woman screaming. You're the only female occupant in the second-floor apartments. Then another neighbor phoned in on their way to work and said your apartment door was wide-open. Holden is there now. He said you're not at home and there are signs of a struggle. Your bedroom and bathroom doors were busted open. There are bullets lodged in your wall."

Crap! How on earth was she going to explain that?

Why was her door open? Had the guy doubled back and left through the front?

"Katie, what's going on? Did you have a break-in?"

"Yep, I did. Some guy wanted…" Should she tell him about the thumb drive now? "Money. A junkie, I think. You remember how one broke into the clinic?"

"Of course, I do. You were scared half to death and reported it yourself, right away. Are you hurt? Are you safe?"

"Yes, yes. I'm not injured, but I'm pretty shaken up with everything that's happened in a short amount of time, and I haven't had any sleep. I'm not thinking clearly. But I'm safe."

"Well, where are you? Why didn't you come into the office?"

Pinching the bridge of her nose, she sighed. "I'm getting a coffee." That sounded completely bonkers. She was attacked in her home and went to get coffee instead of going to the sheriff? *Way to go, Kate.* "Caffeine relaxes me." *It's a stimulant, you idiot.* "You know, uh, I needed something comforting, familiar and a breather to wrap my head around everything."

"Where are you? The café on Third Street? I can have Holden pick you up and bring you into the office. We need to get an official report while everything is fresh in your head."

"No, no need to send Holden." Was she hyperventilating? "I'm actually on my way to your office this very instant. The fresh air will do me good on the walk over."

"Are you at the café?" he asked again.

"Don't worry. See you soon, Jim. You're the best." She disconnected. Quickly, she hit the ride-share app icon to get a lift and plugged in the information for the motel. Her credit card information was already stored in the app.

Dean had told her not to leave, but the sheriff was looking for her, wanting her to come in and file a report after her neighbors had called and Holden went to her place to investigate. Surely, Dean would approve of this change in plans.

She'd barely had a chance to make a copy of everything on the thumb drive, saving it to Dean's computer, when the car pulled up out front and honked. It shouldn't have been surprising that it had taken no time at all, considering there was little traffic and low demand at this hour. But this worked in her favor. The faster she got to Jim's office, the better.

Before heading out into the cold without a coat, she grabbed one of Dean's heavy pullovers, tugging it on over her top and a pair of his leather gloves to keep from freezing.

She had the driver stop down the block from the Albany County Courthouse, where the sheriff's department was located. She thanked him, hopped out into the cold and hurried down Grand Avenue to the large brick building.

Pulling open the front door, she strode inside past the empty information desk. Janeen Phillips, an old friend from high school, worked at the station and would probably be in shortly.

Kate spotted a sign for the restrooms and realized she had no idea how she looked since she'd left the motel in a rush. She stepped into the ladies' room and glanced in the mirror.

At her reflection, she sighed. Her mother would call her a ragamuffin.

Quickly, she splashed some water on her face, used paper towels to dab her skin dry and finger-combed her hair. Mascara and a brush would do wonders, but she had bigger things to worry about. Such as coming up with answers that wouldn't lead to more questions.

Best to just get it over with.

On the walk down the hall to the sheriff's department, she gathered her wits about her.

The courthouse had a faint lemony smell that spoke of cleaning compounds. Oddly, the familiar scent settled her pinging nerves a bit. She reached the end of the hallway and turned left. Two doors down another corridor, she came to an open set of double doors with Sheriff's Department stenciled on the front.

Inside was a long room with a high counter running the length of it. On the other side of the counter were several desks, the dispatch radio and two offices, including Jim's, which was slightly larger than the other.

As Kate approached the counter, a woman in her midtwenties wearing a brown deputy's uniform looked up at her. The deputy's long dark hair was in a tight ponytail that pulled at her features, making them appear sharp, almost severe, and she wore no makeup like Kate, but the younger woman looked fresh-faced, with dewy skin.

She must've been new, because Kate didn't recognize her.

"What can I do for you?" the deputy asked.

"I'm here to speak with Sheriff Ames."

The deputy peered over the top of her computer at Kate. "What's your name?"

"Don't worry about it," Jim called from the doorway of his office. "That's Katie Sawyer. Holden is at her place now."

Good. Holden wasn't there. She'd prefer not to run into him.

"You heard the boss," the deputy said. "Come on through." She indicated a half door at the end of the counter and hit a buzzer.

The door clicked open, and Kate went on through.

"Doughnut?" the deputy offered a box.

The pleasant aroma of sweet fried dough had her stomach grumbling. "Thank you." She pulled off the gloves, grabbed a napkin from the counter and took a glazed one. The first bite was heaven in her mouth. Dessert for breakfast. Whoever invented doughnuts was a genius.

"Want a cup of coffee to wash it down?"

"Bless you, yes," she said around the food in her mouth, now starving. "Just a little cream, please." The sugar from the doughnut was plenty.

Jim greeted her in the doorway of his office. "Morning." Ushering her inside, he looked her over. There was no way his keen eyes had missed the bloodstains on the same pair of jeans she was still wearing. "I see you haven't had a chance to clean up." He frowned at her as he sat behind his desk.

She dropped into a hard wooden chair and set the gloves on the edge of his desk. "The intruder was waiting for me in my apartment after I left the hospital. And he ransacked the mobile clinic, too."

The deputy knocked on the open door as she came in and handed Kate a cup of coffee.

"Thanks."

The deputy went back to tending the front desk.

"Start at the beginning," Jim said. "What time did you leave the hospital, and how did you get home?"

Kate recounted the nightmare, yet again, in between nibbles on the doughnut and sips of coffee until she was finished.

"I'm not clear on how you got away if this man was in hot pursuit after you."

Stalling for time, she crammed the last large piece of doughnut in her mouth and chewed slowly while thinking of a plausible response. "I flagged down a passing car, and it stopped. I got lucky."

"There's so much good luck flowing around I should buy a lottery ticket," Jim said, devoid of humor. "What's the name of the driver who picked you up?"

"I didn't get his name. Good Samaritan."

"You don't know his name, but he gave you his sweater." He gestured to the pullover she was wearing. "Literally, the shirt off his back."

"Like I said, Good Samaritan. I was freezing. I think he was worried about me going into shock."

"Where did he take you?"

"Oh, I had him drive around for a while. Until I calmed down and could think clearly. Then he dropped me off and I got a cup of coffee."

Jim nodded slowly, his jaw twitching from side to side as though processing everything she'd said. "You needed time to let the adrenaline settle and the fear dissipate?"

"Yes, that's it exactly."

"I can understand that, with a guy in a ski mask ambushing you in your home and shooting at you."

"It was terrifying."

"I'm sure it was." He folded his hands in his lap. "So, you were thinking clearly by the time you asked the Good Samaritan to drop you off?"

"Yes." That's what she'd said, wasn't it?

"Then why didn't you come here instead of the coffee shop? This would be the safest place for you to be, wouldn't it?"

Her heart began to slam against her chest.

The sheriff posed an excellent question.

Chapter Eight

Kate took a gulp of her coffee, and the hot liquid went down the wrong way, causing her to choke.

"You okay?" Jim leaned forward.

Clearing her throat, she nodded.

"Do you need anything?"

She shook her head. "No." She patted her chest, ensuring her airways were fully open. "No, I'm fine." What she wouldn't have given in that moment to be a savvy operative. She would've pressed some high-gadget button and disappeared. "You know, recalling it all, I was actually still frazzled when the driver dropped me off. I wanted to collect my thoughts over a cup of coffee. And it's a good thing I did, too, because I found this in my pocket." She took out the thumb drive from the back pocket of her jeans and held it up. "Cheryl must've passed it to me without my realizing."

Jim perked in his chair and opened his desk drawer, plucking something out. "What's on it?" He held open an evidence envelope.

She dropped the thumb drive inside. "I don't know." She squirmed in her seat and caught herself. "I was in the coffee shop when I discovered it. I didn't get a chance to take a look. But I'm pretty sure that whatever is on there is only more trouble if the guy who broke in was after it. I've had my fill for a lifetime." If only she could advertise that to all the criminals in town to keep them from coming after her.

"The decedent didn't say anything to you about this? Explain why she was giving it to you?"

Decedent. The official term for a person who had died sounded so cold and clinical.

"No, nothing. I mean, I didn't even realize that she had slipped it in my pocket."

"I thought you said the intruder was after money. That's what you told me on the phone."

"Did I?"

She gulped and shook her head.

"You also called me Dean." His eyes narrowed as he studied her, hard.

"I was dreaming when my phone rang. Confused."

"Dreaming? In the café?"

Kate chewed the inside of her lip. "Daydreaming. As I was collecting my thoughts."

"About Dean? That Delgado boy who ran away?"

"Crazy, I know. But the shock and the fear had my mind spinning in wild, unexpected directions. I really need to get some rest. I feel delirious at this point."

"Sure." His features softened along with his tone. He held up the bag with the thumb drive. "Obviously yours and the decedent's prints are on here, but we'll check for others."

What?

Kate stiffened, trying keep the alarm flooding her nervous system from showing on her face. She and Dean hadn't had a chance to discuss how to handle this situation, and she hadn't anticipated Jim checking for prints.

Dean's were all over it.

She couldn't catch a break. Every time she thought a predicament had been averted, another popped up.

"The big problem is," Jim said, "we won't get a match unless someone has been fingerprinted before."

Law enforcement officers were fingerprinted—FBI also. Reason suggested the CIA would do the same with their folks.

She clenched her jaw. *So stupid.* Why didn't she think of that?

"Is everything all right, Katie? You look like you're going to be sick."

Aside from the mini nervous breakdown she was having, everything was fine. "I'm not feeling well. The sugar from the doughnut on an empty stomach. No sleep. The trauma of everything."

"That's no surprise. You've been through quite an ordeal in the past few hours. Holden should be finishing up at your place soon. You should go home. Get some rest. I'll have my deputies drive by your way a couple of times each shift to keep an eye out. Make sure you don't have any more trouble." He gave her a quick grin, full of small-town charm.

"I think I'll get a room at a motel. I'd rather not run into Holden." She lowered her gaze. "It's still awkward when we're in the same room." After more than a decade. The only time he treated her like they had no pertinent history between them was when his fiancée, Renee Olson, was present, and she wasn't around nearly enough. It was like he went out of his way to get under her skin.

"I can call him back to the station, if you like, so he won't be there by the time you get home."

She glanced up at Jim and smiled at his thoughtfulness. "No, let him do his job. I don't think I'd be able to sleep there, anyway." That was one hundred percent the truth.

"It'll take some time to get over that feeling, of having your personal space violated. You're welcome to stay with Maggie and me. Colton's room is empty and it's free."

Her smile widened as she stood. "Thank you, that's so generous, but I don't want to impose."

"Impose? Maggie would have my hide if I didn't offer. It's no imposition, truly. I insist."

"To be honest, I think I need to be alone." *With Dean.* They didn't have much time together before he had to leave, and she wasn't going to waste any of it.

"I understand." Jim rose from his chair. "If you change your mind, you know where to find me. Do you need me to give you a lift?"

"Oh, no. I have a couple of errands to run. But I appreciate the offer."

Although her parents had moved from Wyoming to Nebraska to be closer to their new grandchild and help Claire out, Laramie still felt like home. Surrounded by people who'd known her since she was little, who looked out for one another, offered a safe place to sleep or a ride. That was hard to find.

"Any idea when I'll be able to use the mobile clinic again?"

"In a few days, and then I'd recommend using a professional service to get cleaned."

"Sure. Thanks." She hesitated at the door. "Did you happen to find out anything about the mother? Cheryl?"

"Her name was Cheryl Gowdy. Her prints were in

the system. Turns out she was brought in for drug possession eighteen months ago. Since it was only a small amount and it was her first conviction, the judge sentenced her to probation."

Gowdy. The name was familiar, but she couldn't remember where she'd heard it before. "That's it? Nothing else on her? Does she have any family?"

"Her dad's deceased. Nothing else in the file on her. But don't worry, we'll keep looking for other relatives. See if one of them is willing to assume responsibility for the baby."

"Instead of having the deputies swing by my place on their shifts, can you have them stop by the hospital and look in on the baby to make sure he's safe?"

Jim frowned. "They have security guards there. That wouldn't be an efficient use of manpower."

"I know. Please. It'd put my mind at ease, help me to sleep better."

He gave a long sigh. "I'll spread the word to all my deputies. Okay?"

"You're the best."

"I'll let you know if anything turns up on those prints," Jim said.

Heading out of his office, she cringed. How was she supposed to explain that Dean Delgado's fingerprints were on the thumb drive?

This wasn't something she'd resolve on her own. Duplicity wasn't her forte. She stunk at it. Lying to Jim just now had almost given her a coronary.

Dean would have a slick idea on what she should say. Provided he didn't blow a gasket over how she'd messed up first.

At the front desk, she spotted Janeen getting settled in for the day.

"Kate," Janeen said, wide-eyed with a bright smile. "What are you doing here?"

"Oh, there was a break-in at my apartment."

Janeen gasped as a hand flew to her chest. "Oh, my Lord, are you all right? Were you home when it happened?"

"I'm fine. I just had to come in and give the sheriff some information for a report."

Letting out a long exhale, Janeen shook her head. "Thank goodness for that. I'm glad I ran into you, otherwise I'd have to go over to your place and check on you." She looked around and lowered her voice. "Nothing happens in this place that I don't eventually hear about."

"Really?"

Janeen sat in her chair. "Oh, yeah, everything comes through the information desk, whether it's officially or unofficially. Mostly the latter. I see and hear it all." She tapped her long, bubble gum–pink nails on the desk, making an annoying clicking noise.

"You wouldn't happen to remember a girl by the name of Cheryl Gowdy, would you?"

Janeen scrunched her face in contemplation as though she'd never heard the name. "I don't think so."

It was probably a long shot by asking. "A year and a half ago, she was arrested for drug possession. She would have been about eighteen, nineteen at the time. Blonde, around my height, maybe a couple of inches shorter. She was given probation and sent to a halfway house."

Her eyebrows shot to the ceiling with recognition dawning in her eyes. "Oh, yeah, I remember that case because it was so odd."

"Odd in what way?"

Janeen pursed her lips and rolled her eyes. "Well, not so much odd as sexist. They gave that girl probation when ninety percent of the others who come through on a similar charge get jail time. The judge let her off easy because she was a pretty little thing. There was an article about it in the paper and everything. Caused a real stink in these halls. I'm surprised you didn't read it. The story was written by..." Her voice trailed off, and she lowered her gaze.

"Tyler." That was why the name was familiar.

Janeen looked up at her with remorseful eyes. "I'm so sorry. About what happened to him. And for mentioning it like that. I wasn't thinking. My mouth goes a mile a minute, faster than my brain sometimes."

"It's okay." Kate backed away from her desk. "You didn't do anything wrong." Her cell phone buzzed, saving her. "Excuse me." She took her phone out of her pocket. "I have to take this."

"Let me know if you ever want to get together for a drink sometime."

Nodding with a forced smile, Kate turned toward the door and glanced at the phone.

Heathcliff.

"Perfect timing," she muttered under her breath and answered. "Are you okay?"

"I'm fine. I told you I would be."

James Bond always was in the end. "Did you find anything?"

"It's a drug operation. Methamphetamine."

"Just like you suspected." She contemplated telling him about the thumb drive but thought better of it, especially with Janeen within earshot.

The news should be delivered face-to-face anyhow. Might be easier for him to hear if he was looking at her.

"There's a hub on the outskirts of town," he said. "The other location I checked out appeared to be a distribution center. The other coordinates might be more of the same."

Kate pushed outside into the freezing air and shivered, letting the door shut behind her. She'd forgotten the gloves in Jim's office, but she wasn't going back in there to get them. "That still doesn't explain how Cheryl knew to come to me." She walked down the steps. "Who told her I'd help?"

"Where are you?"

She considered telling him she was in the motel room. Lying to the sheriff was one thing. A bad thing. She wasn't in denial over that, but she didn't want to lie to Dean. "Why do you ask?"

"The background noise on your end changed."

She blew out a heavy breath. "I'm in town. Outside the courthouse."

"What?" he said, his voice growing tight. "I told you to stay in the room."

"I know, and I would've. I had just drifted off to sleep when the sheriff called. He wanted me to come in. My neighbors reported gunshots and screaming. One found my apartment door open. I had to come in. I didn't feel like I had a choice."

There was a long pause, and Kate held her breath, wishing she could see his face and tell what he was thinking.

"Okay," he said after an excruciating beat. "I understand."

"You do?" He should be livid, and she wouldn't blame him.

"There's nothing I can do about it now besides adapt and overcome."

Hopefully, he'd feel that way after she told him about Jim running fingerprints.

"I'm ten minutes away. The second location was farther out than I'd estimated. Where should I pick you up?"

She had read all of Tyler's news articles, yet, for the life of her she couldn't recall the one about Cheryl Gowdy. He'd told her something ugly was going on in town but hadn't gotten into specifics, and she hadn't pressed the subject. Half the time Tyler had been chasing conspiracy theories. But the story about Cheryl was legitimate if it had been vetted and printed in the paper.

A thought came to her, and she grimaced with dread. There was one person, at least, who could give her answers—unwillingly, but the woman would talk. Kate was loath to go, but if she wanted to know whether Tyler had been onto something and if it was related to Cheryl, she had no other option.

"Behind the vintage clothes shop on Grand Avenue," she said.

"Why there, of all places? The library would be better. They don't open until ten today. No worries about foot traffic. It's a short walk from the courthouse, and there's a bench in the rear of the building."

Wow, he'd processed that fast.

"I'm heading in the opposite direction of the library. The clothes shop will be closer."

"Where are you going?" His tone slid from curious to mildly annoyed.

She glanced down the street at her destination. "To the *Laramie Gazette*. I have to speak to the editor in chief."

Another pause. "With the woman who was having an affair with Tyler?"

She gritted her teeth. "One and the same."

Chapter Nine

A few minutes after having made up her mind, Kate was walking into the *Laramie Gazette*. As she had expected, Andrea Miles, the editor in chief, aka *the other woman*, spotted her the moment she entered the door.

Their eyes met, and Kate's stomach clenched. The other woman must've been equally uncomfortable, since she went slack jawed as she averted her gaze and hurried into her office, shutting the door.

After Kate had learned about the affair, she'd racked her brain out of curiosity, wondering why Tyler had messed around with her. Andrea wasn't *that* attractive. She had glossy black hair and porcelain skin. An average figure, the same as Kate. Only four years separated them in age—Andrea was older. They were both smart, career-oriented and independent. Maybe he had a professional bond with her that he was unable to share with Kate. Maybe he'd cheated simply because he could.

Even though Kate had never blamed Andrea—Tyler had been the cheater, the one in a relationship, after all—the woman had steered clear of her; she'd even stopped using the services of Loving Paws and started taking her cat to a different vet. Forget about decorum, the loss of a client was the bigger issue for Kate. She needed every one of them to stay afloat financially.

She looked around the open space. Only a couple of reporters were in. Someone could usually be found working almost around the clock.

The story doesn't sleep, Tyler used to say.

Thinking back on it, cataloging the lies, all his late nights probably had less to do with a story and more to do with getting Andrea on her backside.

Straightening, Kate marched to the back of the space to the editor's office. Andrea's head was lowered, her gaze on the computer, her pale complexion florid. Kate rapped on the glass of the door with her knuckles.

Andrea stiffened, not looking up immediately, as if hoping this wasn't really happening. Finally, after Kate knocked a second time, a bit more insistent to show she wasn't going to leave, Andrea raised her head, pasting on a strained smile and feigned surprise.

Attractive, without a doubt. But not *that* much more than Kate.

Taking a deep, affirming breath, she told herself that she could do this.

Kate turned the knob and waltzed in, leaving the door wide-open.

"Morning," Andrea said tentatively, an uneasy expression stretching across her face. "What brings you in?"

"I'm here because I'd like some information about an article."

Andrea blinked, genuinely surprised this time by the direction of the conversation. "About an article?" she repeated.

A weird calm came over Kate. "Tyler wrote one about Cheryl Gowdy. A young woman who was convicted of drug possession but was sent to a halfway house instead."

"Why do you want to know about that?"

"Cheryl died last night. She was with me at the time. There were some men after her. Another broke into my apartment."

Andrea blanched and cast an anxious look toward the office space where the other reporters were. "I don't think I can help you. If you want to read the article that Tyler wrote, I can give you the headline and the date. You can look it up online." Her attention shifted to something over Kate's shoulder.

Kate turned around and gulped. Dean, disguised as DJ, strolled into the *Gazette*. He caught her eye and waved. She gave him a *what are you doing here?* scowl in response.

"Hey, there," he said, approaching her, the issues with his voice modulator seemingly fixed. "Figured you could use a hand." He leaned in and dropped his voice to whisper only she could hear. "You're too nice to do this alone."

Candy-coated. That's what he meant. Not nice.

Kate looked back at Andrea.

The dark-haired woman was staring at them like she was trying to work out a puzzle. "Aren't you the bartender over at Delgado's?"

"He's my friend." Kate narrowed her eyes at her, not caring for the tone of her question or the sneer that had accompanied it. To Dean, she said, "I was just explaining to the editor in chief I need some information."

Andrea folded her hands on top of her desk. "Public information that's accessible to anyone with an internet connection."

"Public information isn't what I'm interested in. I know Tyler was working on something," Kate said, daring to make an assumptive leap. "Was it connected to this article about Cheryl? Was there more to the story than what was printed?"

"I said I can't help you," Andrea snapped. Her lips pinched in a tight line. "Please leave."

Kate stood her ground, crossing her arms, and gave a cool smile. "I'm not going anywhere until I get answers."

DJ cleared his throat. "Ms. Miles, I figure you owe Kate, seeing as you were sleeping with her boyfriend on the down low for months."

Andrea's eyes flared wide, hopefully with shame, and she glanced around the office as if searching for inspiration. Finding none, she swallowed hard and licked her lips.

"Just a few answers," he said, "and we'll be out of your hair."

Andrea shoved away from her desk, her chair scraping across the wood floor, and hurried to the door, closing it. Then she glared at Kate but said reluctantly, "What exactly do you want to know?"

"What was the big deal with Cheryl going to a half-way house?"

"Do you really want to open this can of worms?" Andrea asked.

Kate had already crossed the point of no return. The only way out was forward. "Yes."

Andrea sighed. "If I share what I know, do you agree to leave my name out of it?"

"Of course," Kate said. "I'll never mention you." No reason to involve her further.

Wringing her hands, Andrea took another quick

glance at the two reporters in the bullpen before she went to a file cabinet, pulled out a thick folder and opened it on her desk.

Kate flashed Dean a grin of triumph. He put his hand on her shoulder and gave it a squeeze.

"This is Tyler's research." Andrea flipped through the documents until she found what she was looking for. "Here's the article he wrote. It was supposed to be the first in a series."

Kate took the paper and held it so Dean could read along with her.

The article talked about preferential treatment for young women convicted of drug-related charges. Tyler had used Cheryl Gowdy as his poster girl.

"When it was published, feathers were ruffled," Andrea said. "The *Gazette* received a lot of heat. I received a lot of heat and realized that I might have been hasty in publishing the article because of my personal feelings for Tyler." Her gaze dropped. "I told him I needed better evidence next time if he was going to continue down this road."

Tyler had been stressed out about publishing a story too soon. He had needed support, and rather than giving it, Kate had made an insensitive remark.

Nobody wants anything half-baked. You've got to do your due diligence.

She hadn't even asked him what the story had been about. "Did he find anything else?"

"Yeah, I think he did." Andrea had a forlorn look. "He came to me excited, said that he was working on something major and that he'd been looking at the story about Gowdy from the wrong angle."

Dean shoved his hands in his pockets. "Wrong in what way?"

Andrea riffled through the papers and pulled out a document. "Look at this."

They glanced at the sheet. It was a list of women, eight of them, all under the age of twenty-five, who had been convicted of drug charges. In lieu of jail time, they had been given probation and sent to the New Horizons halfway house.

On the list, there was another name she recognized. "I know her." Kate pointed to one near the bottom. "Lilah Sanchez. She used to come to the clinic with a stray dog that she'd taken in. A cute corgi-Lab mix. I'd treat him for free, and sometimes she'd swing by just to chat. I got the feeling she was lonely, didn't have many friends. But one day she stopped showing up."

"When was the last time you saw her?" Dean asked.

"I'm not sure. Last spring, I think. Maybe late winter. I figured she was busy having fun over the summer and then it was her senior year of high school."

Andrea dug around in the folder and plucked out another sheet. "According to this, Lilah was convicted in March. She repeated an earlier grade and was eighteen at the time."

"Charged as an adult. She could've finished school from the halfway house," Dean said. "These are just more women like Cheryl. This supports his first article, but did he find anything new?"

"All of those women are currently on probation, but none of them are at New Horizons."

"What do you mean?" Kate asked.

"No one in administration would talk to Tyler. He staked the place out for a few days from the time they unlocked the doors in the morning until curfew, when the residents are supposed to be in for the night," Andrea said.

Kate vaguely recalled Tyler mentioning a stakeout, and she also remembered not believing him.

"Those women were never seen entering or leaving the facility," Andrea said. "Tyler eventually found an orderly who would speak with him, only off the record with the assurance of anonymity. That was so like Tyler— dogged, determined." Pride rang in her voice. "The guy told Tyler the women showed up their first week and then he didn't know what happened to them."

"What about their probation officers?" Dean asked.

"Officer," Andrea said, emphasizing the singular. "They all had the same one."

"So, where are the women?" Kate asked.

Andrea threw her hands up with a shrug. "I don't know. Tyler suspected it had something to do with prostitution, but he couldn't prove anything. Yet. He kept digging and was getting close to putting the pieces together. He was so clever. I knew given enough time he would figure it out. Then there was the car accident." She sniffled and wrapped her arms around herself, getting choked up as though his death had been recent. Tears brimmed in her eyes, and Kate handed her a box of Kleenex from the desk. "I know our relationship was wrong," she said, taking a tissue. "Neither of us intended to hurt you, Kate. But it was more than a fling." A whining note of self-pity entered her tone. "We were in love."

That was the reason Tyler had cheated. With Andrea, he'd found a woman who thought of him as clever and dogged and who was the cheerleader that Kate wasn't.

Who had stars in her eyes when she looked at him. Who loved him.

A pang cut through Kate, and she glanced at Dean. The one man she could never forget. The only man she would do anything to be with.

Andrea dabbed at her eyes with the tissue. "After the funeral, I went through his notes, and I was going to follow up on everything, to pay tribute to him, you know." Her voice was raw with emotion. "But one night, I was leaving the office late. I had locked up, and a man wearing a ski mask shoved me up against the wall, put a knife to my throat and told me to forget about the story that Tyler was working on. If I didn't, he would come back and make me regret it before he killed me. That's when I realized that Tyler's accident was no accident at all. I put the folder in the file cabinet and haven't looked at it until now."

Oh, my goodness. Kate actually felt bad for her. Andrea couldn't even mourn publicly as a girlfriend, and after losing Tyler, she had been terrorized and threatened. She must feel so alone.

"I'm sorry for your loss," Kate said.

"Thank you." A surprised note sounded through the tears before Andrea began to cry full-on. It wasn't dramatic sobs, designed to gain sympathy. Her tears were genuine.

Kate was on the verge of cracking and giving the woman a hug.

"Don't you dare," Dean said as if reading her mind. "Tyler was sleeping with both of you at the same time. That wasn't love. It was selfishness and greed packaged in lies."

Andrea's crying dialed down to hiccuping sobs and then petered out. "You shouldn't speak ill of the dead."

"Well, you're alive," he said, shedding his casualness like a second skin. "You knew he had a girlfriend and that they were living together. Why did you do it? Was it low self-esteem, lust, you simply didn't care? All of the above? But don't stand here and tell her you decided to become the other woman because of love."

The realization of how much Kate had confessed to Dean over strong drinks, the intimate details, made her want to shrivel up like a slug in salt. Thank goodness she'd always insisted on using a condom with Tyler. She'd never fully trusted him or loved him, and she hadn't wanted an *oops* baby tying them together for the rest of their lives.

"And," Dean continued, clearly on a roll, "while he was two-timing you, Kate, you were giving this one—" he hiked a thumb at Andrea "—a thirty percent discount because she was his boss."

Her overweight Burmese cat had needed surgery, too. Kate did a quick calculation of how much money she'd lost on those discounts, and it made her blood boil over the bills she could've paid off.

This woman did her owe her, in more ways than one.

Dean's hard gaze swung back to Andrea. "Any idea who was the last person Tyler interviewed?"

"Uh," she stammered, blinking wildly, thrown for another loop. "The day before his accident, he pushed the probation officer for answers." Sniffling, she dabbed at her eyes. "But she stonewalled him."

"She?" Kate asked. "Who is their probation officer?"

"You shouldn't pursue it," Andrea said. "Tyler was killed over this. It's dangerous."

"I appreciate your concern." Kate believed it was sincere. "But we need a name."

Andrea pursed her lips. "You don't mention me to anyone, or Tyler, because it will only lead back here."

Dean gave a quick nod. "Agreed."

"The probation officer is Renee Olson."

Shock jolted through Kate. "Holden's fiancée?"

"Like I said, you didn't hear any of this from me."

Chapter Ten

Sitting behind the wheel of his Jeep, Dean looked at Kate over in the passenger's seat. She had the thick folder in her lap, clenched in her hands. She was still shaken and processing things, but they needed to discuss what they'd learned.

"Do you think Holden is involved with what's happening?"

"I don't know." She dropped her head into her hands. "I hope not."

"It would make sense if he were. Having an insider in the sheriff's office would be smart. Someone to keep their finger on the pulse of things, keep her out of trouble, make evidence disappear. How long have Renee and Holden been together?"

"I'm not sure. A couple of years, I think. He proposed on Valentine's Day." She blew out a heavy breath. "Is it possible Holden killed Tyler? I mean, even if he's not directly involved in whatever Renee has going on, what if he murdered him to protect her? Holden would do anything for somebody he loved."

"There's a big difference between self-defense and cold-blooded murder of an innocent man. Would he go that far?"

She threw her head back on the seat. "I don't know, okay!"

He put his hand on her leg. "Okay. You know him better than I do after all this time."

"Not really. Things are strained between us. Awkward."

"Why? Back in the day he was such a good guy, and you two were friends. So close sometimes it made me jealous."

"I don't want to get into it." She pushed his hand from her thigh. "You don't have the right to pop up after fifteen years and start asking questions about friendships and grudges and the interpersonal dynamics of everyone. Not when I don't know diddly squat about you. Or what your life is like now, or who your friends are."

"Just to clarify, do you have a grudge against him or is it the other way around?"

She growled at him, teeth bared, eyes crazed.

"All righty," he said. The phrase made him think of his mother. She used to say it from time to time.

He would miss his mom once he left again, but the one positive about her Alzheimer's was that she wouldn't remember that he'd been there. She was too far gone. Didn't recognize anyone from her past these days. He'd made friends with her as DJ, and that had been enough for him. More than he deserved.

"Do you want to know about my life?" he asked.

Kate stilled. "Yes."

"The CIA team I've worked with for the last decade, Hunter, Zee, Gage, they're my only friends. The nature of our work was classified, and the missions were hard and required a lot of time away from home. Over the years, we became close. Tight-knit. They're family to me. Being without them is like missing an arm or leg. It's weird. I've worked so hard, made so many sacrifices for this country, I never thought it was possible for me to be in this position. On the run. Branded a traitor. I feel lost."

He had no idea where all of that came from, but now it was out there. The truth.

"What about your real family?" She shifted in her seat, facing him. "Your mother. Your brother."

He ached to yank off the stupid mask he was wearing, but they were still in town, and he didn't want to take unnecessary risks. "By the time I found out my mom had cancer, she'd already gone into remission and then she'd been diagnosed with Alzheimer's. And Lucas..." Dean huffed a breath. "He wants nothing to do with me. Won't talk to me. Barely looks at me."

"What about me? No phone call. No email. No snail mail. You never looked back. Did your new family simply replace all of us? Is Zee your girlfriend? Or is there someone else?"

Clenching the steering wheel, he wasn't sure how to make her understand. "My mom, Lucas, *you*, none of you are replaceable. And no, Zee isn't my girlfriend." She was brilliant and bombshell beautiful, but she was like a sister to him. "There is no one else. Never anyone serious. I haven't been free to have a real relationship."

"Because of the demands of your job. The traveling and secrecy."

"No." He shook his head. That was a part of it, but a small part. "You think I've never looked back. Are you kidding me?" He gave a sharp laugh that ended in a piti-ful sigh. "All I do is look back, to the point where I can't move forward. Because when I left you behind, it was like ripping out my heart." He'd been living as the Tin Man for the past fifteen years.

She stared at him, her eyes filled with sadness and uncertainty. She was weighing his words, trying to decide if he was telling the truth.

Not that he blamed her. He'd spent the past nine months lying to her face, pretending to be DJ.

Her cell phone rang. She pulled it from her pocket and looked at the screen. "It's the sheriff. Which reminds me, I have some things to tell you."

Great. "Go on, answer it."

She hit the speaker button. "Hello."

"Hey, Katie. I hate to bother you. Hopefully you weren't sleeping."

"No, I was awake."

"I need to locate DJ. I tried the number he gave me, but it didn't go through. I contacted the motel he was staying at, they knocked on his door and at my insistence they went into his room. It looks like he cleared out of there. Do you happen to have a good phone number for him?"

She slid a furtive glance in Dean's direction. "No, I'm sorry, I don't. We're not close like that. He's just my friendly neighborhood bartender."

"Okay. Well, if you hear from him, please have him contact me as soon as possible."

"Will do." She disconnected.

"What did you need to tell me?" Dean asked her.

"I gave the sheriff the thumb drive."

"Did you save the information first?"

"Yeah, I thought of that. What I didn't account for was that he's going to check the drive for prints. Yours will come up."

Was that all? "Not in his database. He'll never know about me. It'll ping the CIA, but I'm sure they already know I'm here."

"Moot point?"

"Pretty much."

"One less thing to worry about." Her shoulders sagged, and her gaze dropped to the folder Andrea had given them.

"Penny for your thoughts."

"Lilah. She's the only apparent thing that would explain the connection, why Cheryl chose me, who sent her." Kate looked up at him. "It's just that Cheryl had bruises on her legs like she'd been abused. The thought of Lilah, or anyone, for that matter, going through whatever horror Cheryl must've endured is a lot."

Dean resisted the urge to think about wretched memories of his own.

"Do you think it's true, about the prostitution?" Kate asked.

"Probably. I overheard talk from a couple of the guys in the bar. Ugly rumors."

"When are rumors ever the pretty kind? No one whispers about good things. What did you hear?"

"Talk about buying sexual favors."

"You mean at a brothel?"

"I didn't catch the specifics." He started the engine and put the Jeep in Drive. "But I know who to ask."

Ten minutes later he parked at the Ranch and Home Supply store across town on Snowy Range Road.

"What makes you so sure Mr. Sanders will talk?" Kate asked.

"Trust me, Ed will talk. Sit tight." He left the engine running and hopped out. Inside the store, he glossed over the aisles of supplies and headed to registers at the far end of the store.

"Morning," Ed said with a grin on his beefy face, his thinning gray hair slicked back, as he stocked a shelf. "I'm surprised to see you in here, DJ. This is my wife, Betty."

The middle-aged woman operating the register didn't smile, but she did tip her head in acknowledgment.

"Can I speak to you a minute?" Dean asked. "In private."

Ed frowned. "Sure." He wiped his hands on the smock he was wearing and led the way over to a feed area where bags of food were stacked.

No one was within earshot.

"I've been in town awhile," Dean said, "and I'm looking for some female companionship."

Ed's frown deepened. "Not sure why you're coming to me. Betty doesn't have any sisters I can set you up with. We're both only children. But there's Friday night bingo at the church. Plenty of widows that go every week."

"I was thinking someone younger. Someone I could *pay* for a couple of hours of company."

Ed froze, flushing darkly. "I don't know what you mean." His anxious gaze darted to Betty.

"Really. 'Cause I think you do. I've heard you talking in the bar. Come on, help me out."

The flush faded as abruptly as it had come, leaving him pale and sweating. "I'm not sure what you're implying, but I don't appreciate it." He cast a swift glance over his shoulder back toward his wife again.

"The implication is clear. I'm not judging. I'm just looking to get in on the action."

His wife was eyeing them at this point. No doubt wondering what they were whispering about.

"How much longer do you think you have until the Mrs. comes over?" Dean asked. "I'd hate for Betty to hear anything about this."

Horror filled Ed's eyes. "Okay, okay," he whispered. "I've only been once. The place changes location every week, but it's always somewhere near Rawlins, Casper or Cheyenne."

Ed knew a lot for a onetime customer.

"How do you know where to find them?" Dean asked.

"Craigslist. Under *Missed Connections* and then *Cleaning Pipes*."

Was he serious?

Considering you could find a hit man on Craigslist, if you knew precisely what to look for, it wasn't too surprising prostitution was being advertised there, but the search terms were a bit too on the nose. "How much should I expect to spend?"

"Fifty to two hundred. Depends on what you're looking for."

"Are they open now? Do they provide round-the-clock service?"

"How the hell am I supposed to know? Fellas tend to go at night. Now get out of here." Ed scurried away and resumed stocking the shelf.

Dean left the store and climbed back in his vehicle.

"Well, did you find out anything?" Kate asked.

"Yeah, he talked. But I think it's best to wait for nightfall to check out what he told me."

"What do we do until then?"

Dean pulled out of the lot and hit the road. "We'll swing by your place so you can grab some fresh clothes,

and I'm sure you need to eat. I'm starving. After that I
need to take a look at Craigslist."

"Craigslist? Whatever for?"

"Missed Connections."

Chapter Eleven

While Kate was in the bathroom taking a shower, Dean unbuttoned his top and removed the padded belly from over his T-shirt. He washed his hands and face and toweled off.

He had rehashed his conversation with Ed as they'd eaten takeout from a café. It only took minutes for him to verify the information. He'd looked up Craigslist and had found the advertisement just as the man had described. There wasn't any mention of sex, of course. Or fees. Not a word about young women. The only indication there was something odd, and that it wasn't an advertisement for a plumber, were the coordinates.

Dean went back to the laptop and searched the spreadsheets she'd copied from the thumb drive to see if there was a match on any of the sites. Sure enough, the coordinates were on the data sheet. Figures varied on a weekly basis between the location and two others.

In addition to the prostitution ring, they were more than likely running drugs through those sites also. Made sense. The guys who showed up there were interested in partying, probably inebriated, and if not already drug users, then at least they'd be more susceptible to try a narcotic in that environment.

Those sites were a two-for-one money maker.

The bathroom door swung open, letting steam and the scent of Kate's body wash escape—warm vanilla and a hint of pear. Fresh-faced with no makeup, she stepped into the main room, dressed, a towel in her hand, drying her hair. She sauntered to the bed and sat beside him.

She smelled good. Looked good.

So beautiful.

"You took off the fake tummy." She slid her hand along his torso, her fingers lingering on his abs, and every muscle in his body tensed. "Did the CIA give you all that stuff?"

"It's CIA issued, but *give* would be an inaccurate representation." Technically, when he went on the run, taking the disguise with him, he'd stolen it.

She was still touching him. Her hand roamed up his chest, fingers splayed wide, over to a shoulder and down his biceps. "You've been hiding a lot under those clothes." She grinned, and her smile shot right to Dean's core, and the tension that had been a part of him for the past decade and a half, the knot that was so tightly coiled every waking minute, eased.

"Want to watch TV?" He got up and crossed the room. "I can put on something to take our minds off things." He looked around on the dresser. "Where's the remote?"

"Right here." She picked it up from the table and strode over to him.

He reached for it.

But she pulled the remote back. "I don't want to watch television. I want to finish our earlier conversation."

They'd talked about a million things. "Which one?"

"The one where you said leaving me behind was like ripping out your heart."

The ground shifted under his feet just enough to let him know diving back into emotional territory, in this motel room, with a bed a few feet away, and her smelling and looking so irresistible, would not be prudent. "I don't know why I told you that."

Her brow knitted. "Was it true?"

"It's true." And there was no denying the feelings for her that were deepening with every breath.

She set the remote down on the dresser and looked up at him with the most intense stare he'd ever seen on her. They weren't touching, and yet, with their proximity, he felt heat radiating from her, felt the curves of her body close to his. He ached to haul her into his arms.

Get a grip.

Aching for women wasn't his style. Yet, here he was, staring into Kate's eyes, longing to brush the hair from her face and reel her closer.

"Why did you leave?" Her voice was a whisper. "No lies. No evasion. Just tell me. I need to know."

"Things had gotten unbearable at home. I knew that if I didn't leave, it was going to be me or *him*. My stepdad. I'd lie awake at night, bruised and hurting, thinking about how to kill him."

"Dean." Horror contorted her features.

He'd dreaded seeing that look from her. That was one of the reasons he'd never told her.

After his dad died, the bar had fallen on hard times. His mother had remarried, to give her boys a father and as a way to survive financially. When his stepdad had been sober, things had been fine. Then he got injured on the job and hurt his back. Taking Vicodin for the pain had led to drinking. And when he drank, he became mean. Violent. A different person. Eventually, it seemed like he was drunk more often than he was sober.

"I couldn't continue in a constant state of fear and pain, with my mother making excuses for him. And I didn't want to end up in prison for killing that bastard. So, I left."

She stepped closer, putting a palm to his chest. Her touch soothed something deep inside him. "Why didn't you take me with you?" she asked, softly.

"How could I take you with me? We were seventeen. Underage. Your parents would've had the cops on us so fast. And I didn't have any money. No real plan. I ended up living on the streets, getting my GED, picking up odd jobs until I was old enough to join the Marine Corps without parental consent."

"But you never contacted me. Why?"

The truth wasn't pretty.

The truth sucked.

But if that was what she wanted, needed, he'd give it to her. "I was lost, trying to rebuild myself. In here." He covered her hand on his chest with his own. "If I had rushed contacting you, we probably would've gotten married, and I would've messed up your life. I had to make something of myself to give you what you deserved." Tears filled her eyes, and he brushed damp hair from her cheek, tucking the strands behind her ear. "By the time I had gotten my life in order, had my head on straight and settled at the CIA, it felt like too much time had passed. That I had missed my chance. I thought for sure you were in a relationship with someone else. That you would've forgotten me."

She reached up and touched his cheek. "I could never forget you."

His heart swelled. His body was drawn tight with

desire and need. His head was a tangled mess of guilt and love.

Love for this one woman that had never died, despite the time and distance.

"The worst part was," she said, "deep down, I don't think I ever stopped waiting for you to come back to me."

He slid an arm around her waist as he buried his other hand in her hair. Staring at her, all he could think about was kissing her senseless.

Actually, kissing wasn't the only thing on his mind.

Rising on her toes, she closed her eyes and leaned in and then his lips were on hers.

Her mouth was soft and hot and eager. She kissed him deep and hard, like she never wanted to stop, rubbing her soft curves against him, sending a rush of heat to his groin. Her body was so sensual, so addictive. He took another greedy kiss and another, dragging her closer, falling deeper with each breath he stole from her lungs, with each moan of pleasure from her that he swallowed.

Desperate need took over, and in it, he found that heat, that sense of urgency they'd always had together.

His mind spun, intoxicated by her, his thoughts tumbling to how he'd looked her up and gotten her contact information. To all the phone calls he'd resisted making, the emails he'd typed and deleted. To how he had thrown himself completely into work to force himself not to think of her, to ignore the loneliness, even though he knew his heart would always belong to Kate.

But what must it have been like for her?

It wasn't until then he realized he was cupping her breast, stroking her supple flesh with his thumb.

Drawing back, he tore his mouth away, and they both gasped for air.

He wanted more. A lot more. The need to touch her everywhere, to take her until they were both boneless and exhausted, was a pulse throbbing in his entire body. But it wouldn't be right. Not when he had to leave again.

"We shouldn't do this." He stepped back. "We should stop."

Her rich brown eyes grew wide. Her rosy lips parted, the lower one trembling. "Why?"

"It seems like a good idea right now. But in the morning, when I have to leave, and in the days to follow, I don't want you to think back on this and regret it."

"That's assuming the kill team doesn't find us and we live to see another sunrise."

"This isn't a joke." They weren't in any imminent danger, but the threat was real.

"Who said I was joking?"

"I don't want the memory of me to keep causing you pain."

"It's not the memory of you that hurts. It's being without you. Because I'm still in love with you." She squeezed her eyes shut for a heartbeat and then looked up at him again. Determination burned in her eyes. "I have never wanted anyone or anything as much as I want you. Make love to me, Dean. Don't say no. Not when it's what we both want."

Arousal gripped him like a fist. Fortunately his brain was still functioning—barely, but it was working—and it warned this would be a mistake.

HER FACE, HER whole body, flamed. The truth had poured out of her. Like a dam breaking with no way to stop the deluge.

She could see the war going on in his face. The need

to do the right thing. The desire to be with her, even if it was only for one night.

For months, he'd been watching her, talking to her with that glint in his eyes. One she had ignored, thinking he was elderly DJ, but with Dean staring at her like that, she understood what that gleam meant.

He ached for her the way she ached for him.

Over the years, she'd tried to forget him. Had taken drastic steps, such as moving in with Tyler, to force herself to get *over* him. Now he was here, in this room with her, and suddenly the world seemed full of possibilities that she actually desired. For starters, stripping off his clothes and getting *under* him.

He sucked in a sharp breath as though her touching him was torture.

She could tell his last bit of control was fraying, so she pushed it further. Ran one hand up his neck, across the stubble of his jaw and tangled her fingers in his hair. The other hand she slid lower, over his tight abs, and lower still, where she palmed the hard bulge that was proof of his desire.

"You're not playing fair," he groaned.

Well, if this was a game, she had every intention of winning.

"Funny, I never had to work so hard for you to take off my clothes when we were teenagers." She crushed her mouth to his and took what she wanted.

He tasted so good. So *familiar*.

This man set her senses on fire. He was the flame and she was the moth. She didn't care if she got burned. Not if it meant she could have him again, even for a little while.

In the moment of his surrender, he kissed her back,

and their tongues tangled together. His arms swooped around her, bringing her body tight to his as he pushed her up against the wall. The release of his self-control seemed to ignite an insatiable need he'd been keeping locked down, and she melted against him.

"Tell me," she said, taking a ragged breath. "Tell me you want me." She felt it in the sureness of his lips, the heat of his tongue, in the roughness of his hands on her body, but there was something special about hearing the words.

"Yes, I want you." He went after her mouth again in a deep, all-consuming kiss.

Winning never tasted sweeter, and she couldn't get enough of him.

She loved that he no longer showed any of the reluctance he'd expressed earlier. His mouth on hers was hungry and impatient, and his hands were equally demanding as they roved over her body. She matched him in every single emotion, stroke for stroke.

She tugged the shirt over her head and tossed it as he did likewise with his.

He slid the straps of her bra off her shoulders, along her arms, and pushed the lace cups down.

Trembling under the heat of his gaze, she thought about her body. How it must look compared to when he'd last seen it. No longer seventeen and lissome and effortlessly lean. Her body was thirty-two. She wasn't sure how much it had changed since then, because she didn't pay a lot of attention. All she knew for certain was that she couldn't squeeze into her jeans from high school, she ate more cheeseburgers than salads and her idea of strenuous exercise was walking to the kitchen for a glass of wine.

"Let's turn off the lights." She reached for the lamp.

But he caught her wrist, stopping her. "Why?"

"Time has had an effect on all this." Lowering her gaze to the floor, she gestured slightly from her breasts to her hips. "It's not the same cute, *tight* teen bod you remember," she said with a nervous giggle.

"Time has had a great effect. I'll take gorgeous over cute and girlish any day." He dropped her wrist and took her face in his palms, forcing her to look at him. As he held her gaze, his eyes changed in a way that made her wish she could fall into them, swim in their fathomless depths forever. "You're so beautiful. More beautiful than before."

The sincerity of it had her rocking back, staring up at him, lips parted, enjoying way too much how that made her feel.

One of his hands lowered, curling around the side of her neck, bringing her closer. The feeling of his strength, his heat through that simple touch made her want him even more.

"If we're going to do this," he said, "I want to see you. All of you."

Oh, they were definitely going to do this, and after what he'd just said, the lights no longer mattered.

She took in the sight of him.

Time had had an astounding effect on him as well. Gone was the boyish work in progress. Now, he was solid muscle. Taut and sexy. Ripped in a way that made her want to enjoy every inch of him. He looked like a dream come true.

"Okay. Lights on." She wanted to see him, too. *All* of him.

A dirty grin tugged at his mouth. With his thumb on

her pulse and his palm on her nape, he brought her mouth to his. His other hand caressed her exposed breast and thumbed her nipple. He squeezed it in a not-so-gentle pinch and rolled the peak between his fingers.

The contrasting sensations of his hot, tender kiss, his tongue gently caressing hers, along with his rough hands sent her hormones into overdrive.

Stumbling across the room, they copped feels and kissed as he managed to unclasp her bra and tug her pants off along the way. They fell to the bed, their arms locked around each other. He was only in jeans with the button on his fly undone, and she was in nothing but panties.

She'd missed this. The excitement, the passion, the raw intimacy of being with Dean. But he was no longer a boy. He was all man now and had the body to match. She explored him with her fingers and mouth, memorizing the feel of his chest hair against her skin, his nipples tightening on her tongue, the carved ridges of his abdomen contracting at her touch.

Needing more of him, of everything, she lowered his zipper and slipped her hand down his pants, to find him rigid and thick and long. But then he was kissing his way down her body. The next thing she knew he'd stripped off her panties.

Ripples shot over her as his mouth found its target between her thighs.

His tongue, his fingers—it was incredible. *So, so hot.*

She hadn't expected this, but sometimes the best things in life were the ones you didn't see coming.

Driving her fingers into his hair, she encouraged whatever he was willing to give. She'd take it and give back double. She was close, right on the edge when he took his mouth from her and nipped her inner thigh.

"More?" he asked, his tone playful.

No more games, this was serious business. "Yes. Yes," she begged, squirming as though she was trying to get away while her hands in his hair tugged him closer.

He resumed what he'd been doing, knowing how she wanted to be touched. The knowledge, learned with time and care—something she hadn't received in a long while—was an intimacy so much greater than simply coming together.

With his hands and mouth revering her body, she felt safe. Desired.

Her body squeezed at the surge of his tongue, as if to capture and hold it there, and then his magic fingers had a tide of release rolling through her.

She dug her heels into the mattress, her hips lifting as wave after wave of sweet heat engulfed her. He drew out the sensations, feeding on her pleasure.

"You taste even sweeter than I remember," he said, low and husky.

As soon as she recovered, able to breathe again, she happily reciprocated. Pushing his back to the bed, she took him in her mouth. Licking, sucking, kissing, stroking until he was the one begging.

"Kate, please, *Kate*," he muttered. "Stop, honey. I want to be inside you."

Grinning at the feminine power she still had over him, she crawled up his body, planting kisses along the way.

He rolled them, flipping her under him.

Under was so much nicer than trying to get *over*.

"You have protection?" she asked. This wasn't a matter of trust or love. They hadn't been together in fifteen years, and although he might not have fallen for anyone else, a man this hot had not been a monk.

With a nod, he was moving. A second later, he pulled a condom from his wallet.

Just as she thought. He was prepared.

Climbing back on top of her, he made quick work of the wrapper and slipped it on.

He lowered his body, his hips settling, forcing her legs to spread wider, and buried himself deep in a single thrust. They both gasped at the first stroke of their joining.

"You fit me like a glove," he groaned, rocking into her, steady and hard, and her intimate flesh stretched and pulsed around him.

Everything else ceased to exist. There was nothing but the two of them—no worries for tomorrow, no regrets for yesterday—just this splendid moment, together.

She turned her head to the bedspread, and her lips parted as she went soaring. "Dean," she cried out in another long breath.

"I know." He turned her face back to his. "I'm right there with you." His gaze stayed locked on her for a second before their lips met again, their tongues tangling.

She loved how much Dean kissed while he made love to her. The feeling of his mouth, his tongue, the feeling of *him* on top of her, inside her... She screamed her release.

His rhythm increased, growing harder and faster, and he followed her over the edge with one last thrust and a guttural groan of pleasure.

He glided his lips up her neck, along her jaw and up, where he caught her mouth in a sweet kiss. She held him, kissing him back. Strung out following the most intense orgasm of her life.

Rolling off her, he kept her with him, holding her close in a tangle of limbs. They shared the same air as they caught their breath, their hearts pounding together, neither of them willing to relinquish the intimacy for space.

"It's only ever been you," he said, low and husky. "I love you. Still. Always."

This happiness was sublime, almost a miracle. At the same time, it was frightening. Fragile as a soap bubble that might burst any second.

She wanted to freeze this moment. Both quivering and sated. His body next to hers, his fingers curled in her hair, his mouth pressed to her ear, his breath warm on her neck. She'd think back on this, replaying each tiny detail, when he was in Canada or Mexico, miles away, and the terrible loneliness gnawed at her. She shoved the thought from her mind.

For now, she would revel in this, the two of them laid bare, skin to skin. Heart to heart. Where they belonged to each other and *this* one thing in the world was perfect.

Chapter Twelve

As much as Dean hated putting that stupid mask back on, he was loath to leave Kate behind in the motel even more. He'd never forget the feel of her body molded to his, the ecstasy of being inside her. The pleasure of simply being with her.

She was special. Look at what she had accomplished with her life. A veterinarian who owned her own practice. That wouldn't have happened if he had contacted her at eighteen, straight out of basic training.

The CIA had picked him up right before his first enlistment had ended and changed the course of his life. Apparently, his scores on certain aptitude tests made him a good fit.

If he had reconnected with Kate while he had still been in the marines, who knows where either of them would have ended up?

He was certain he would've ruined her future. Limited her opportunities.

Kate was a triple-threat kind of woman: bighearted, beautiful and unafraid to do the right thing.

Making love to her had been more incredible than he'd dreamed.

He had no idea why she'd been self-conscious about

her body. She was sexier than before, fuller breasts, rounder hips. An hourglass figure he would've worshipped all night if he didn't have to drive out near Buford to investigate *Missed Connections*.

Fortunately, it was only a twenty-minute ride.

The satnav chimed that he had almost reached his destination. He was approaching slowly. Now off-road, the terrain was a bit bumpy.

There were lights about two hundred yards ahead. In the surrounding darkness, he made out the shape of a small structure.

As he drew closer, the Jeep's headlights cast the building in enough light for him to see what it was. A tiny house. One of those portable homes that could be hooked up to a heavy-duty pickup and moved without much fuss at the drop of a dime.

He parked a few feet away from an SUV and a motorcycle. In front of the tiny house was a Ford F-250. A tough-looking guy sat behind the wheel with the engine running and headlights off, paying attention to his phone. He must've been a bodyguard for the women.

Armed with zip ties and duct tape, Dean alighted from the vehicle.

The tough guy hopped out of the truck and jerked his chin up in greeting, his nose piercing catching the light. He was big. And tall. Maybe six-five.

"Hey," Dean said, keeping his hands in his pockets.

"What are you interested in?"

"Looking to get the pipes cleaned."

"Want any *ice* for your party?" he asked, referring to the meth.

"Nah, I'll pass."

"What about a little booster to help you along, old-timer?" The guy took out a small plastic pouch filled with blue pills. "One will make sure you get your money's worth. Only fifty a pop. You'll last for hours."

For one pill? That was highway robbery. Not to mention what those poor girls had to endure. "Thanks, but I don't need any help in that department."

"Suit yourself." He hit a button on his phone and put it to his ear, speed-dialing someone. "Got one coming in."

A second guard was inside. A good thing Dean hadn't taken this one out prematurely. It would've alerted the other to trouble.

The guy disconnected. "All right, have fun."

As he turned to hop back in the warm confines of his truck, Dean made his move.

Jumping on him, Dean snaked his legs around the man's waist, his right arm over his throat.

Panic made the guy start bucking. He dropped his chin to block Dean's elbow.

Dean whacked him in the back of a head with a palm strike, which weakened him just enough. Quickly, Dean gripped his forehead and tugged back to let his elbow snake underneath the guy's chin. The choke hold was locked in place. Dean had him now.

It was only a question of time.

The man staggered while Dean held steadfast before dropping to his knees, and then it was lights out. Dean zip-tied his wrists behind him, restrained his ankles and put duct tape over his mouth.

He dusted off his jeans and hurried to the door. Through the glass windowpane, he spotted the other guard sitting in a chair, reading a magazine. He opened the door and stepped inside, closing it behind him.

Putting down the magazine, the guy stood. "DJ?"

Dean flinched. He hadn't counted on being recognized, and now that he had a good look at this one, he knew him as a regular at Delgado's. "Hey."

"This your first time?"

"Yeah, it is."

"Here are the rules. You let the girl know what you want, she'll give you a price. If you party without paying, she lets me know and then I have to hurt you. If you rough her up, then I really got to hurt you. Break an arm or bust a kneecap. Other than that, have fun. Got it?"

"Sure, I got it. Is Lilah available? I heard she's sweet and would be good for my first time here."

"You're in luck. She is free. Room number three."

"Thanks."

Not wasting any time, Dean decided to go for the man's throat but with a frontal attack. He bent his right arm and slammed his forearm into the man's Adam's apple. The guy made a wheezing noise, and the struggle was over right there.

Dean restrained and gagged him.

With the guards handled, he took a look around. As far as tiny houses on wheels went, it was huge at about forty feet long and ten feet wide and tall enough for an upper level. They must've needed a special permit to transport it on the road. The house had been specifically designed to be a brothel rather than a home. Beyond the front door, there was only space for a couple of chairs. There wasn't a living room. No kitchen. No dining area. The rest of the structure contained six bedrooms, three on the bottom and three on the top level. In the rear was a full bathroom and kitchenette—a sink, counter space for a hot plate and mini fridge.

What these guys were doing out here was abhorrent.

But from a design aspect, the setup was ingenious. No rent to pay, no land or deed in someone's name. The portability of the structure was a huge advantage for staying under the radar and avoiding unwanted attention.

Still, his stomach turned.

From the male grunting noises and fake sounds of female pleasure, he knew rooms one and two were occupied with clients.

He went to the room marked number three. After a quick rap on the pocket door, he slid it open.

The room—more of a six-by-eight cell—had a full-size bed with barely enough space to walk around it. No closets. No windows. One little nightstand. A young woman, a girl of eighteen, with mousy brown hair and sad eyes, dropped a book on the floor, pulled out earbuds and turned off an MP3 player. She sat up on the bed and opened a robe, revealing her naked body.

Dean averted his gaze and turned his back. "Please, cover yourself."

"Don't you want to party?"

"I want to talk."

"That's a first."

"Are you covered?"

She sighed. "Sure."

Dean stood on the threshold, where he could keep tabs on the clients and see if anyone else approached the entrance. "Get dressed. I'm getting you out of here," he said in a low voice.

"We're not allowed to leave the premises. Sorry."

"I'm a friend." Dean met her confused gaze. "Do you know Cheryl?"

Lilah jumped to her feet. "Yeah. Is she all right? Did she have the baby?"

"Kate delivered the baby. A boy. You were the one who sent Cheryl to her, weren't you?"

Lilah nodded.

"What's going on here?" Dean asked. "Why are you women here instead of at the New Horizons halfway house like you're supposed to be?"

She swallowed hard and bit her lower lip.

"I can be trusted," he said, keeping his voice low. "Kate trusts me. She wanted me to come and help you. Please tell me what's going on."

She peered around Dean into the hall. "What about the guards?"

"I took care of them."

Lilah looked him up and down. "You did?"

"Yes. Now before someone else shows up, tell me."

"The story is the same for all of us. We got arrested and convicted on drug charges. Sentenced to probation at New Horizons. Our parole officer—"

"Renee Olson?"

Lilah nodded. "She said we had a week to find a job. Nobody in town would hire us. Not that we were given much time. When the week was up, Ms. Olson told us that she found us a job in hospitality. Either we took it or we went to jail. We jumped at the position, not realizing it was going to be here, working on our backs. Once we arrived, they pumped us full of drugs, wouldn't let us leave."

He glanced back at the hall. By the sounds of it, at least one man had finished. "Listen, we can't talk properly here. I'm going to get you and the other girls out."

"They won't let you take us."

"They're in no position to stop me. I can get you and the others someplace safe. Do you think they'll come?"

Her eyes widened as she chewed on her lip. "There's nowhere safe." She shrank back, looking terrified. "They'll find us, and when they bring us back, there'll be hell to pay."

If he took seven women to Laramie or Cheyenne, the news about them would spread faster than fire through dry underbrush. He still didn't know if Holden was involved, who was behind this operation or the lengths they'd go to in order to silence these girls. "What if I took you out of state?"

"Are you crazy? We're all technically on probation. We get caught over the state line and we'll go to jail for violation of our parole."

"This prostitution ring is illegal. What you're being forced to do is wrong. Would you and the others come if I got the FBI involved?"

"The FBI?" She crossed her arms, her gaze falling, like she wasn't sure if that would make the situation better or worse.

"The FBI will protect you while they investigate."

"The feds won't help. They won't believe us. To them, we'll only be a group of lying hookers."

"This particular fed is my cousin." Getting him involved was the right decision, but Dean would have to be careful on how he handled it. "He'll believe you. This racket that Renee Olson has roped you vulnerable women into is horrible. If you don't take a stand, take a chance and trust me, then she'll keep doing this to other women."

Lilah rubbed at her arm, as if it hurt, her features pinched tight with stress. Her sleeve slid up, and he spotted a purple bruise. Finally, she said, "You're right. They'll never let us go. Not with what we know. They'll keep using us until they can't anymore, and then they'll trap others as replacements. The way they trapped us."

One of the other bedroom doors slid open. Dean could hear a man speaking.

"Get dressed," he whispered. "Start rounding up the others while I take care of these guys."

She nodded and darted to her clothes that were hanging on a hook.

As the man stepped into the hall, shutting the door, Dean swept up on him, easily subduing him and throwing on zip ties and a gag.

Lilah was dressed and made her way up a narrow flight of stairs to the upper level.

In the first room, the client was still going at it. Little did he know that he was done.

Dean wrenched the door open.

"Hey!" the man screamed, a startled look falling across his face.

Dean grabbed the guy by the hair and yanked him off the brunette beneath him. The woman scrambled to cover herself.

Without bothering to let the man dress, Dean kicked his legs out from under him. One punch and he was out cold. After binding him as he had the others, he dragged the man to the front and put him beside the other two.

Lilah rounded up the women, giving scant details and promises of safety. On their way out the door, they searched the men's pockets and took any money they could find.

While the women crammed into his Jeep, Dean pulled his knife from the glove box and flattened the tires on the tiny house and every other vehicle.

Provided those men got loose, he didn't want to make fleeing the area easy for them.

Starting his Jeep, he counted six women. "I thought there were seven of you out here."

"There used to be," Lilah said from the passenger's seat. "But one girl tried to run. They chased her down like she was a dog and brought her back. They hurt her." A hand fluttered to her throat. "Made us watch."

In the rearview mirror, he glanced at the women in the back. Some nodded. One looked out of it, like she was high. The rest sniffled, huddling together, gazes lowered.

"Then they killed her. Shot her. Made us dig the grave and buried her in an unmarked hole," Lilah said. "That's how we were all going to end up. Used. Beaten. Murdered."

This had to stop, and he was going to do what he could to put an end to it.

Dean took I-80 going east. They could be in Fort Collins in an hour. He'd take the women to a local women's shelter he knew, run by a church. Call his cousin. Explain everything. There was no way his cousin would resist the bait: justice, a career-making case, saving lives, helping family. Once his cousin showed at the church, Dean would bolt. They couldn't have any face-to-face contact. It could compromise his cousin and himself. Dean had no way of knowing whether he was aware of his fugitive status.

After his cousin heard firsthand confirmation from these women, Jake would be hooked. To ensure his commitment, Dean would overnight the folder of research from Andrea and the information from the thumb drive. With documentation plus witnesses, there was no way Jake wouldn't pursue this.

"What about Cheryl?" Lilah asked. "Aren't we going back to Laramie to get her? We can't leave her behind."

Dean clenched the steering wheel. "Cheryl didn't make it."

"Oh, God." Lilah gasped, gripping the door handle. "They killed her," she said, and the women in back whimpered and started crying. "Did they hurt the baby? Did they kill him, too?"

"Two men showed up at the pet clinic, but I took care of them. They're dead."

"*You* took care of them?" one girl asked.

"Looks can be deceiving," Dean said. "Those men didn't hurt Cheryl. She died in childbirth. Kate did what she could for her, but in the end, there were complications and she hemorrhaged."

Silence descended. The women stilled, exchanging looks.

"What about the baby?" one woman in the back asked. A redhead.

"He's alive," Dean said. "Healthy."

Lilah exhaled in relief and sagged down in the seat.

"Why did those men want the baby?" Dean wondered. "Was it to use him as leverage, to keep Cheryl quiet?"

"You better explain," Lilah said to a woman in the back.

"Okay." The redhead nodded. "Last year, before Lilah joined us, Cheryl and I and a couple of the other girls were taken to a party. In Cheyenne. A lot of bigwigs. Powerful men were there. We were supposed to be the entertainment. The host took me and Cheryl down to this sex dungeon. Did weird things to us. Cheryl was a better actress than I was. He took a liking to her. Started seeing her over and over again. Sometimes two to three times a week. So often, she didn't have to entertain regular clients. Then she got pregnant. She swore it was his because he was the only one who refused to use protection. Once she started showing, things got tense. They moved her into an admin role. Had her keeping track of the books, making drug runs, that sort of thing. One day she came to us, crying. Said they were going to take her baby. And if it turned out to be *his*, she'd never see the child again."

His?

"Cheryl told us she stole information that would protect her and the baby," Lilah said. "Damaging stuff that would make them leave her alone."

"Who was the bigwig?" Dean asked. "Who did Cheryl think was the father?"

More hesitant looks were exchanged in silence.

"You have to tell him," Lilah said. "He needs to know if he's going to help us."

"Lyle Kingsley," the redhead said, and the name rang a chilling bell. "The governor."

Chapter Thirteen

"You're my official hero," Kate said to Dean, sliding her thigh in between his leg as they nestled in bed.

"I don't feel like a hero. I feel like I did the bare minimum to help those women."

That's what made him the perfect hero, and he didn't even realize it. Sought no glory. No thanks. No pat on the back for a job well done.

Well, she'd shown him her thanks for the past hour in bed, and now he just looked completely wiped out.

"When you called your cousin to explain everything, did you tell him about the trouble you were in?" she asked.

"Not exactly, but Jake suspected something was up because I refused to meet with him face-to-face. I didn't want to risk getting him into trouble."

"Will the women be okay?"

"The shelter at the church had room for them, but that'll be temporary. Once Jake puts all the pieces together, he'll be able to get them into the witness protection program. They'll have new lives somewhere else."

"You did a great thing tonight."

"Only because of you." He kissed her forehead. "You were right to want to pursue this."

She was, but at what cost?

"If the governor is involved, maybe even Holden…" Her thoughts whirled down the rabbit hole again, her brain spinning like the little blue circle on her computer screen, struggling to keep up.

"You won't be safe," he said. "Not until there are convictions and those responsible for orchestrating this are put behind bars. Lilah will tie you to Cheryl. I was identified at the brothel. Well, DJ. And there's a known connection between us."

"I was thinking the same thing." She hesitated, trying to summon the nerve. "I want…" *You. I want to be with you.* She swallowed past the tightness in her throat. "I want to come with you."

"What?" He leaned up on an elbow and looked down at her, his dark eyes unreadable.

"Disappear with you. For a while, anyway. Until it's safe. I don't mean you'd be stuck with me forever. I was only suggesting—"

He tugged her onto her side, bringing her into his body, and touched his lips to hers. Tender and firm. "I didn't want to presume that you'd want to leave with me. I'm a fugitive. It'll be dangerous."

"You'll protect me. We'll keep each other safe."

"What about your business, Loving Paws?"

"I'm in the red." She had hinted things weren't good, but she had never divulged how bad her financial situation was. "I'm struggling to survive as is." Giving discounts certainly hadn't helped.

"I don't want to mess up your life by taking you with me."

"I'm not seventeen." She shoved away from him and sat up, drawing the sheet along with her to stay covered.

"I'm capable of making my own decisions and living with the consequences of my choices."

"Hey," he said, sitting up beside her. "That's not what I meant. I'd be lucky to have you with me. For however long you wanted. I love you, Kate. I only want you to be safe and happy."

They sat there, staring at each other.

Maybe she shouldn't have suggested it and waited for him to broach the idea.

"Stop it," he said. "It wasn't a mistake to mention it. I wasn't going to. I'm too terrified of wrecking your life, of still being the wrong guy for you. My situation is worse now than it was fifteen years ago. How's that for irony?"

"I would've left with you back then." She turned to him and leaned against his chest. "Even if I had to live with you on the streets."

"I wouldn't have let you. I would've swallowed my pride and groveled at the door of my cousins in Fort Collins. I would've worked five jobs, done anything to spare you from that."

"Don't you see, that's why we'll be okay. Together." They had a rare kind of love where they would sacrifice anything for the other person. "But I'm still worried about the baby. Especially if he might be proof of the governor's illicit actions."

"Jake knows about the baby, that his DNA could be evidence. There's security at the hospital. And the sheriff is aware that men were after Cheryl and the child. I think he'll be safe."

"The sheriff did agree to have his deputies swing by the hospital on their shifts to check on him. But what if Holden is involved? What if he goes to the hospital?"

"The Holden I used to know would never hurt a kid. I

get that you two aren't on the best of terms and it's possible he killed Tyler, but do you really think he'd hurt a baby?"

Holden could be a jerk at times, but he wasn't evil, soulless. "No, I don't."

"He's going to be okay. Trying to make a baby disappear with so much attention already drawn to him would bring serious heat no one would want."

She lay back down. He was right beside her, tucking her close, his skin hot, his muscles dense and solid. She burrowed against him. It felt so good to be wanted like this, to be held. They stayed that way for as long as they could.

The sun was already up.

"We need to get going," he said and headed for the bathroom.

"What about your mom? Are you going to say goodbye?"

"I've been debating about that and whether it's worth taking the chance." He started the shower and came to the doorway. "She doesn't remember me. Not as an adult."

"But she knows DJ. It's incredible how you became friends with her." Kate had never given DJ's visits to the nursing home a second thought. He'd mentioned being a family friend of the Delgados, and it seemed only natural for him to stop by and see her twice a week. The fact he had managed to forge a genuine relationship with her, a friendship, was not only beautiful but also impressive.

"I didn't expect her to take to the disguise, the persona." He leaned against the doorjamb and crossed his arms.

"But she did. Don't squander this opportunity to say

goodbye. The guise doesn't matter. You don't know if you'll ever get a chance to see her again."

"That's true. It weighs on me, how I left before. Not saying goodbye. I thought one of you would try to talk me out of it, convince me to stay, and I knew how that would end." He sighed. "I'll swing by the nursing home to see her one last time. Any loose ends you want to tie up?"

"I think I need to tell the sheriff about what's going on."

"That brings us back to Holden."

"All the more reason he needs to know. Holden is his top deputy. I have to give the sheriff a fighting chance, so he doesn't get a knife in the back." Or a bullet.

"Do you want to take my backup gun with you?"

She was a good shot. Her dad had made certain of that. But it was broad daylight, and she was going to be in the center of downtown. "No, I don't think I'll need it. I'm going to hit the bank and speak to Jim while you're visiting your mom. I'll wait for you to pick me up at the café."

"Then we hit the road. Together."

"I like the sound of that."

"Want to join me in the shower?"

She smiled. "Just to wash up?"

A devilish grin hitched his mouth. "We can get dirty again before we get clean."

She liked the sound of that, too.

CHEWING A PIECE of gum, Lucas sat alone, low in the back seat of one of the three SUVs that had been waiting for the team when they landed last night. Going to Kate's apartment had turned up nothing. Apparently, she'd run into some trouble. Her mobile pet clinic was a bloody, ransacked mess, and there were bullet holes in the bathroom wall of her apartment.

A search of hotel records for her name had given them zero results.

Lucas was certain she was with Dean. The only question was where?

Since he was in charge and the one calling the shots, he had half the team surveilling Kate's place in case she came back. The odds were good that she would return if she had left in a hurry. The other half of the team he'd sent to Nebraska to see if she and Dean had gone to her parents' place.

Two days ago, he never would have thought an operative such as Dean would risk going somewhere familiar, expected, yet, the target had shown up here. Their hometown, of all places.

Target. Not brother.

Using binoculars, he stared at the entrance of the Silver Springs Senior Living and Memory Care Center through the front windshield. Sitting in the back seat, rather than behind the wheel, made it easier to go undetected. Anyone driving by wouldn't notice him, their eye trained to scan the front seats. The only reason to sit in the driver's seat was if you had to give chase quickly or make a hasty getaway.

Lucas kept his gaze on the entrance.

Dean had proven he wasn't big on sentimentality and saying goodbye. But Kate was. If they were together, as he suspected, her influence would hold a lot of sway over him.

It was a long shot he'd show up here, but one worth gambling on. The only other option was to simply wait and hope for another facial recognition hit on him. Going that route was a recipe for failure.

He was hedging his bets on Silver Springs and Kate Sawyer's influence.

Lucas took out his phone and dialed the front desk.

"Hello, this is Lucas Delgado," he said, well aware that the kill team were watching and listening to everything through a device disguised as a button on the collar of his shirt. "I'm the son of Miriam Delgado as well as her agent, fiduciary, for all matters concerning her."

"Yes, Mr. Delgado. If you'd like to speak with Miriam, she's eating breakfast right now."

"No, I don't want to disturb her. I'd just like to know who her visitors have been over the past six months."

"One moment and I'll take a look for you." There was the clack-clack of typing on a keyboard.

A Jeep came down the street. A Renegade. That was the third time it had passed. The very same one. Lucas was certain of it. But this time, it turned into the Silver Springs parking lot.

"She's only had three different visitors," the attendant said. "Lourdes Delgado."

His cousin, Lola, from Fort Collins, who managed the bar.

"Kate Sawyer."

That was nice of her to check in on his mother. Kate was that kind of person. Thoughtful. Sweet.

The Jeep pulled into a spot and parked. The driver stayed in the vehicle a moment, checking his mirrors.

"And DJ. Davis Johnson."

Bingo. "Could you describe him for me? A Latino guy in his early thirties with dark curly hair?"

"No, not DJ," she said, with a smile in her voice. "He's

in his late seventies. White. Gray hair. A full head of it, too."

"Any identifying marks on him, such as tattoos or scars?"

"Um, none that I can recall. But there is one distinctive thing about him. He always wears latex gloves. He has OCD."

I bet he does. OCD about leaving his prints behind.

The driver got out of the Jeep, an elderly gentleman matching the description. He hit the key fob, locking the Jeep, and Lucas caught sight of his hands before he slipped them in his pockets.

Latex gloves.

Well, I'll be damned. "Speak of the devil."

"What's that?" the attendant asked.

"Nothing. Thanks for your time. You've been very helpful."

Lucas stabbed the red icon, disconnecting the call, and took out a case from his canvas duffel bag. The contingency kit was smaller than a fishing tackle box. Inside were a myriad of different GPS trackers—among other things—designed to be hidden on vehicles, in clothing, inside a cell phone case.

Smiling, he grabbed one for a vehicle.

A CRAWLING SENSATION skittered down Dean's spine again. Like spiders on his backbone. That feeling wouldn't leave him—that he was being watched.

He hastened his steps, darting a quick glance over his shoulder.

Nothing.

He'd even taken the precaution of circling the block

twice before pulling into the lot to be sure it wasn't being staked out by a team. He'd spotted no one.

The doors to Silver Springs whooshed open and a warm gust of air greeted him. It was convenient that nursing facilities were prohibited from imposing *visitation hours* on the residents. They were free to have visitors at any hour, in theory, provided the resident hadn't withdrawn their consent.

Dean strode inside and went to the front desk. "Good morning," he said.

The attendant hung up the phone and looked up at him. "That's so funny. Speak of the devil is right."

"What do you mean?"

"I was just talking about you."

An icy chill shot through his blood, making the hairs on the back of his neck prickle. "About *me*? To who?"

"Oh, it was just Miriam's son. Lucas. He was asking about her visitors, that's all."

Damn it.

Maybe he should turn around and leave. The CIA must've had Lucas making calls from Langley, trying to get a bead on him.

If a kill team was already here in Laramie—possibly here as in outside those doors—there was nothing he could do to change that fact. Taking sixty seconds to say goodbye to his mother wouldn't alter his odds of living or dying.

Sixty seconds, then he was gone.

"Where is she?" Dean asked. "In her room?"

"In the dining hall. I'm sure she'll be happy to see you."

Dean hurried down the hall and around the corner, with his hand squeezing the butt of his nine-millimeter in his jacket pocket. Weekday mornings had always been the best time for him to visit her. The bar was closed, traffic was light and there were usually only the residents and staff.

Entering the dining hall, he spotted her. Three tables over sitting alone. Her silvery-gray hair was in a single braid down her back, and she sat with a bowl of oatmeal in front of her. As soon as she saw him, her eyes lit up.

"DJ!" His mom smiled and waved.

He hurried over to her table. "Hi, Miriam. You're looking lovely as ever."

"Oh, stop it." She laughed and clutched his arm. "I wasn't expecting you this morning. Did you bring me anything?" she asked, looking to see if had a bag in his hands.

Usually he brought her a breakfast sandwich or a pastry. Anything he knew she'd enjoy. Today, he'd been in such a rush, he'd forgotten to swing by the café after he dropped Kate off.

"Sorry. Not today."

Her smile fell, but the light didn't dim in her eyes. "That's okay. I guess it's oatmeal for breakfast after all. Sit down."

"I can't sit this morning." He put a hand on her shoulder and crouched down beside her, so he kept physically low in case a sniper had a line of sight through the windows, and where he could spot anyone entering the room.

"If you stay down low like that, you might not be able to get back up." Worry washed over her face.

"I'm fine. I've got good knees."

She grinned. "Lucky you."

As much as he hated to admit it, he was going to miss this. Seeing her smile. Their fun little chats. Playing cards together. Being her friend after years of being angry and frustrated, disappointed, in her choice to stay with their stepdad.

Back then, he didn't understand that the decision couldn't have been simple or easy for her. She didn't have any skills or a degree. Delgado's Bar was all she had left of their dad, of his dream to be a business owner. Leaving the marriage while staying in that small town, when their stepdad owned a piece of the bar once he bailed it out of trouble, when his name had been put on the mortgage after they refinanced, it would have been a living nightmare for her.

There was no such thing as a reasonable negotiation with someone drunk, mean and violent.

"Something has come up, Miriam. I have to leave town today. Right now."

"Oh, no." Her shoulders sagged.

"I want you to know that you're an incredible woman," he said, and she beamed. "I know you were a devoted mother. That you love your children, and I'm sure they love you, too. I'm sorry your eldest, Dean, left without saying goodbye. He didn't mean to hurt you."

Confusion swam in her eyes. "Did I tell you about Dean?"

"I love you. More than you know. I'll miss you and I wish I had done things differently."

She put her palm to his cheek, and her expression changed, her brows drawing down. "Your face feels strange. The texture is—"

Rocking on his heels, he drew back, away from her hand. It was the first time she'd ever touched his face, the mask.

"Weird," she said after a beat.

A whistle sliced through the air in the room. The sound mimicked the call of a cedar waxwing. He didn't need to look up to know who it had come from. Years ago, he and his brother had used that whistle to signal to each other that their stepdad was drunk and the other should run and hide. Or that the coast was clear, and it was safe to come home.

Lucas was in Laramie. In Silver Springs.

Dean stood, drawing his gaze up.

"Isn't this nice." Lucas strutted over to the table. "We're having a family reunion."

Chapter Fourteen

The line at the bank had been so long, she would've thought it was payday. Kate didn't close her account, not wanting to draw suspicion. What little money she had she withdrew. All of her debts and bills she'd have to sort out when she could. Her landlord already had her last month's rent, and she wouldn't see a dime of her security deposit.

But none of that mattered. She was going to be with Dean. *Finally.*

Kate crossed the street and entered the courthouse. The same lemony scent hit her, relaxing her the tiniest bit. She had no idea how to explain to Jim. Accusing Holden of anything would be a bad start. There was no proof he was involved, and she wasn't going to presume his guilt by association with Renee.

"Hey, there," Janeen said. "Twice in one week. Consecutive days, no less. It's a sign we should get together for drinks. How about tonight at Delgado's? You just have to walk down the stairs from your apartment."

"Wish I could, but I've got a lot going on these days. Maybe some other time." Kate hurried past her and to the sheriff's department.

The station was abuzz with activity. It was a reasonable hour and three other deputies were in, including the brunette with the severe ponytail.

"Is Sheriff Ames in?" Kate asked her.

"No, he's out," she said.

"But I'm here," a male voice called from the other side of the room. Holden stood, leaning on the doorjamb of the smaller office. A smug smile was on his face. His arms were folded across his chest, and his legs were crossed at the ankle.

The entire department fell silent. It was quiet enough to hear a pin drop. Everyone's gaze bounced between them.

She didn't need this today. "That's okay." Kate edged back toward the door. "I can speak to him another time."

"Don't be a scaredy-cat. Come on." Holden gestured to his office with his head. "I won't bite."

All those gazes swung to her.

She *so* did not want to do this.

"I could make you come into the office and talk to me," Holden drawled. "If I had questions about your statement regarding your intruder."

The sounds of a clucking chicken blasted in the room, coming from someone's computer or phone. The male deputies snickered.

"Real mature," she said with her eyes narrowed. *Jerks.* She went to the half-open door and pushed through after the buzzer rang. "Thank you." She tipped her head to the female officer, who hadn't been laughing at her.

"Okay," Holden said to the deputies, "knock it off."

The clucking stopped. Thankfully.

She brushed past him into his office.

He closed the door and strode around behind his desk, taking a seat. "Sit," he said, as if issuing a command.

"I'll stand since I won't be staying long."

"You're always avoiding me."

Because he always acted like a blockhead. "Sorry you feel that way."

"It's the truth. The sheriff told me you didn't want to go home because I was at your place."

"What questions do you have about my statement?"

"None." He leaned back in his chair, a grin tugging at his lips, and put his feet up on the corner of his desk. "What do you want with the sheriff?"

She gritted her teeth. This was exactly what she meant. He loved going out of his way to get under her skin. "I had asked him to have the deputy on shift swing by the hospital and check on the baby. Cheryl Gowdy's son. To make sure he's all right. I wanted to see how the patrols were going. If there was any trouble."

"Patrols?" he scoffed. "They've got security guards at the hospital. What's so special about this kid that he needs protection anyway?"

"The men that were after Cheryl had threatened her and the baby."

"You mean the dead men?" he asked slowly, purely for effect to make her feel like an idiot.

"Yes, but they might've been part of a gang or something."

Holden blew out a heavy breath. "The sheriff isn't going to waste that kind of manpower. Even if the request is coming from you, princess."

She squeezed her hands into fists. "Did the results come back on the paternity test? To see if one of the dead men was the father?"

His face darkened in a scowl.

To think she had once been attracted to him. He was

good-looking, in that all-American, blond hair, blue eyes way. Tall. Strapping. But his personality had become so ugly.

"I don't know anything about that," Holden said. "The sheriff probably had it run through the morgue. At the hospital. Is there anything else, your highness?"

"Yeah, what exactly is your problem with me?" she snapped.

"Do you really want to know?"

"Yes." It wasn't a rhetorical question.

He set his booted feet on the floor with a thud and stood. "You don't know how to treat people."

"Excuse me?" She always minded her manners. Said "please" and "thank you" and went out of her way to help others.

He hooked his thumbs in his utility belt. "You heard me."

"If you don't want to tell me, fine." She turned on her heel to leave.

"You never gave me a reason."

She spun back around, bewildered as to what he meant. "Huh?"

"The night before prom. You dumped me. In a text. No explanation. Nothing. I drove out to your place and you were too yellow-bellied to face me. Remember?"

Of course she remembered. It hadn't been one of her finer moments. She'd been depressed over Dean and wallowing in self-pity. But that had been fifteen years ago. "Are you still holding a grudge about that?"

"We were friends before we started dating." He put his fists on his hips. "Good friends. I always had a thing for you, and when Dean disappeared, I was more than happy to be your shoulder to cry on. For months, I listened to you go on and on about him. Deep down, I knew that you might never love me like you did him. He was your first and all. But I figured that it had to count for something that I was the one there for you when he wasn't."

It was as if the wind had been knocked out of her. For a long, interminable moment, she couldn't speak. Only stared at him. "Holden, I…"

"I was a good boyfriend."

"Yeah, you were." The best a girl could ask for back then. Considerate. Affectionate without being handsy or pushy. Holden had been the sweetest.

"But I wasn't him. So you ghosted me."

She lowered her gaze to the floor, unable to look it at him because it was true.

"I didn't deserve to be treated that way. Like I meant nothing," he said, his voice low and soft. "Nobody does. You should know that better than most. Instead, you turned around and did to me what he did to you. For a while, I thought it was me. Something I had done. Then I noticed your pattern." His tone turned cold. "You did the same thing to every guy you dated."

Her head snapped up, and she stared at him. Had he been keeping tabs on her? Did he have a logbook of her dating activity?

"You would've done the same to Tyler, too, if he hadn't died."

Mortification doused the flames of her anger. "Are you finished shaming me?"

"Yes."

"You're right. I never thought about it that way." Not until she saw it through his eyes. "I'm sorry I waited until the last minute to bail on prom." If she had given him enough notice, there would've been plenty of other girls who would've gone with him in her place. "I'm sorry I hurt you and never gave you an explanation. You did not deserve that."

None of the guys she'd dated had.

Holden drew in a deep breath and stepped closer. "Was that so hard?"

Yes! "No. Are we good now?"

He extended his hand. "Water under the bridge."

She accepted the truce and shook his hand.

"You don't have to avoid me from now on," he said. "I won't give you any more grief."

"Thanks." She rolled her shoulders. "Being with Renee must've driven you to hash this out with me."

"I guess so." Holden shrugged. "Maybe it was just time for us to clear the air."

"How long have you two been together? I mean, how well do you really know her?"

Holden narrowed his eyes, and she immediately regretted the question. "Well enough to ask her to marry me. Are you about to give me a new reason to hold a grudge?"

"Nope. I've got to run." She edged to the door. "It was good to chat with you." The resolution was one weight off her shoulders, though the situation with his fiancée was the size of a boulder and still bearing down.

She skedaddled from the office without appearing to flee. On the way out of the building, she threw one last wave to Janeen.

The plan was for her to meet Dean at the café. She headed down Grand Avenue, her hands stuffed in her coat pockets, her head down against the wind. Two blocks away from the coffee shop, someone called her name from the street.

"Katie, there you are."

She halted to see the sheriff in his vehicle stopping alongside the curb. Relief poured through her. "I could say the same. I was just in your office."

He held up the gloves she'd forgotten in his office. "Hop in out of the cold."

She opened the door and climbed inside.

"I'll drop you at your hotel. Which one are you staying at?" He pulled off, cutting into traffic, and headed down the street.

"Oh, that's not necessary. Really."

"I've been looking for you. Actually, I'm still trying to find DJ. I need to get his statement about what happened the other night." He took a left, going in the opposite direction of the café. "The hospital said he was never examined. At this point, I'm worried he may have suffered a head injury. Could have lost consciousness."

"I'm sure he's fine. You shouldn't worry."

"Have you seen him?"

"Uh." She lowered her gaze to her hands in her lap and realized how guilty that must appear. She forced herself to look up. He turned onto South Corthell Road.

Where was he going? This was the scenic route, whatever the destination.

"I haven't seen him," she said.

"Do you have a good phone number for him? A way to contact him?"

Her gaze dropped again. *Darn it.* "I don't," she said, meeting his gaze. "Sorry. I, um, I think he left town."

Jim pulled over and stopped the vehicle. "When did he leave?"

"I don't know." She glanced around. They were

parked near the barren field on Corthell. No other traffic. No sidewalks with pedestrians.

"Where did he go?"

"I, um, I don't know." She looked out through the window. There wasn't a soul around.

"Then why do you think he left?"

Unease slithered over her. "He mentioned something in passing." She clutched the door handle.

Jim hit a button. The locks engaged. "Katie, I know you're lying to me."

She pulled on the handle, but the door wouldn't open. Panic bubbled up inside her. She yanked harder.

"Child safety locks on," Jim said.

"Let me out." Her racing heart dropped into the pit of her stomach. "I'm supposed to meet someone."

"Who? DJ?"

"No."

"Maybe Dean Delgado."

She froze. "No."

"There you go, lying to me again," he said in the disappointed tone a father would use with a child, but something in his voice made her skin crawl. "You've been lying a lot lately."

He pulled a resealable bag from the door pocket. A piece of cloth was inside.

"Open the door, Jim." She yanked on the handle again, knowing it wouldn't open. "Let me out!"

He pried open the bag, and a sweet smell, similar to ether, wafted out. "Afraid I can't do that. My property was stolen last night. And I want those girls back." Jim pounced, shoving the cloth into her face, and pressed hard against her mouth and nose.

With each panicked gasp, she sucked in that sweet

smell. She swung at him, hitting his arms, landing a fist to his face, but he was stronger, so much stronger than her.

The strength leached out of her limbs, and then searing darkness swallowed her.

Chapter Fifteen

Dean stared at his brother and tightened his grip on the gun concealed in his pocket.

Likewise, Lucas had his right hand shoved in a coat pocket with a distinct bulge. "The only one missing from this get-together is Kate."

Miriam looked between them, confusion clouding her eyes. "What's going on?"

"Hi, Mom. It's me, Lucas." He stepped up to the table.

Dean tensed. He didn't want to shoot his brother, hurt him, but if he was part of the team sent to put him down, execute him, then Dean would do what he had to. Wound his brother to get past him.

"You're not Lucas," Miriam said. "Lucas is a boy. My sweet, cute boy. I don't know you."

"That's what you said to me, at Langley." Dean put his finger on the trigger but kept the gun in his pocket.

"What?" Lucas asked. "Did I call you cute and sweet? I don't think I did."

"You said you didn't know me. That your brother was dead."

"Brother?" Miriam asked, glancing between them. "You two can't be brothers."

"I have to go now," Dean said to her while staring at Lucas. "I love you, Miriam."

Lucas scrunched his face in a sad-puppy-dog look. "How touching."

"Will I see you again?" Miriam reached for his free hand.

"I don't know."

"Don't count on it, Mom," Lucas said. "Dangerous men are after him. He's going to have to take a trip. No return visits allowed."

"Do I know you?" Miriam asked again. "You seem familiar, but…"

Dean kissed her temple and stepped toward Lucas, angling the muzzle of the gun toward him.

"I come in peace." Lucas pulled his hands out of his pockets and raised his palms. "I mean you no harm."

"Yeah, and I'm Santa Claus."

"Where are you hiding your sleigh and reindeer?"

"Walk." Dean put a hand on his shoulder, turned Lucas around and shoved him toward the door. He checked his brother's pockets. No gun. Only a candy bar. "What's this?" Dean asked holding up the candy instead of the gun with attached sound suppressor he'd expected.

"Breakfast of champions. Don't judge."

Dean kept them walking toward the exit with Lucas in front of him. "What are you doing here?"

"Saving you. Even though you don't deserve it."

"How many men are waiting outside?"

"None."

Dean pressed the muzzle of the gun into Lucas's kidney. He had no intention of shooting him, if he could avoid it, but he wouldn't fatally wound him. "Try again. How many?"

"On my life, on Mom's life, there are no men waiting outside to my knowledge."

"Funny, I don't believe you."

"I heard what was happening. That you'd been found. Here in Laramie. I had to come."

"Why?"

"To help you."

"Why?" He pressed the muzzle deep into his back. "I'm nothing to you. Your brother is dead. Remember?"

"After what you did, leaving me behind to deal with everything on my own, if anyone is going to kill you, then it should be me."

That Dean believed. "This is how we're going to play it. I'm going to use you as a human shield. If a single shot is fired in my direction before I'm safely in my vehicle, I put a bullet in you."

"All righty. Sounds fair."

Dean's heart clenched as his thoughts flashed to his mother.

It was hard not to think about the teenage boy he'd left behind. His sweet, funny brother, who had to deal with the chaos and the fear and the violence all by himself.

In the lobby, Dean stopped before the motion sensors triggered the entrance doors to open. "Is the kill team waiting outside?"

"All I know is that one was dispatched. Destination Laramie. I would be shocked if they didn't have boots on the ground before me."

Dean shoved Lucas against the wall, throwing one forearm under his chin and putting the muzzle to his belly.

The front desk attendant was staring at them, but he didn't cast a glance in her direction.

"I didn't lead anyone here to Silver Springs," Lucas said. "Mom is in both our files, so they know about her. But I didn't spot any surveillance. Only you." Lucas held his gaze, and it didn't waver. "You circled the block twice before pulling into the lot on your third time around."

Fear whispered over Dean. His kid brother had found him, surveilled him, and he'd been none the wiser. "Why are you here?"

"Do you think I want you getting shot down in front of Mom? We've never even talked about it. What you did. What happened while you were gone. What I went through. You don't get an easy out with a slug to the head by some kill team."

Dean believed that, too. "Move." He shoved Lucas forward. "Let's see how many friends you have waiting outside."

Lucas didn't fight it. With his hands raised high on either side of his head, his brother did as he was instructed.

The doors whooshed open. Freezing air washed over them, but Dean's blood was so heated with adrenaline he barely noticed the breeze.

Peering over his brother's shoulder and using him for cover, Dean remained in a position where a sniper—if there was one—couldn't take a shot. He was waiting for any men who might be close by to make a move.

There was nothing but the wind.

"Let's go. To my vehicle. Quickly. If you run, I shoot you."

Lucas hustled to the Jeep Renegade while Dean ducked behind him, moving in time with his step. Dean kept his eyes peeled for movement, for any sign of danger.

Still, nothing. But the quiet, the stillness only amplified that niggle in the back of his brain that this was wrong. Off.

If Lucas was here, surely a kill team wasn't far behind him.

At the vehicle, he had to let go of Lucas's collar to grab his keys. He hit the fob. The doors unlocked. "Where's your vehicle?" Dean asked.

"Across the street. Black SUV."

Dean took a peek. "Looks like standard government issue."

"More like standard rental issue. It was that or a beast of a truck, because there was no way I was getting a sedan."

Dean shoved Lucas away, hopped in his Jeep and cranked the engine.

"You're going to need my help!" Lucas called to him.

Pulling out of the spot, Dean rolled down the window. "The day I do it means hell must've frozen over." He tore out of the parking lot and bulldozed across the street. Taking aim at his brother's SUV, he shot out two tires.

Lucas was yelling something at him with his arms thrown up in the air, clearly peeved, but Dean was not taking the chance of having his brother follow him.

Pressing down hard on the accelerator, he raced down the street toward downtown. He whipped out his cell phone and dialed Kate. It rang and rang and rang. Voice mail picked up.

His pulse pounded, his heart banging against his ribs. He waited a couple of minutes before trying her again. Each second drove his blood pressure higher.

He ripped off the mask, tossing it into the passenger's seat, and scrubbed a hand over his face.

Her line rang twice and was answered.

"Thank God, Kate." Relief flooded him. "I was worried sick when you didn't pick up the first time. Did you get your money? Are you ready to leave town?"

"Sorry, Katie can't come to the phone right now," a man said. A voice Dean recognized.

Jim Ames.

Dean's stomach twisted and roiled as he pulled off onto the shoulder and stopped.

"No need to clam up now. You were so chatty a second ago, Dean Delgado. Or should I call you DJ? Or is it *Heathcliff*?"

Dean was shocked into stillness.

"Yeah, I know who you are," the sheriff said.

"How?"

"That doesn't matter right now. What does matter is that I have Katie. You stole something from me last night. Six girls, to be specific. I want them back. Return them to me and you can have Katie."

Emotion welled in the back of Dean's throat. "If you hurt her, I'll kill you." The words came like broken glass.

"In two hours, I'll call again to give you a location. You'll have twenty minutes to get there and make the exchange."

His mind whirled. The women were an hour away in Fort Collins and already on the FBI's radar. His cousin had interviewed them last night. Taken statements. Not that he would ever hand them back over to suffer again. But he needed time to think. To strategize.

"I can't do it in two hours. That's not enough time," Dean said.

"It had better be, for Katie's sake."

The line went dead.

Dean beat his fist on the steering wheel. He fought through the rage and the fear surging inside him and pushed through the red haze clouding his mind. That bastard had taken Kate, and Dean couldn't just sit there, spinning his wheels. Not when she might be hurt.

Even if he showed up with the women, there was no way that dirty sheriff was ever going to let Kate and him simply walk away. Not with everything they knew. The meeting would be someplace where Ames would have the tactical advantage. Where he could have armed men hidden and waiting to strike. No telling how many thugs he had at his disposal.

Dean would be walking into a trap, outmanned and outgunned.

Hauling in a deep breath, he forced himself to focus, and that's when it occurred to him that all the coordinates from the thumb drive were only in Albany County. The sheriff's jurisdiction. He should've dug deeper into a possible link between the sheriff's department and the drugs and the prostitution.

Too late now.

All he could do was find a way to get Kate back and keep them both alive.

As if a kill team and his brother weren't enough to worry about.

An idea came to him. A bad idea. One that might end up being a colossal mistake.

But what other choice did he have?

Lucas kicked at the flat tire and swore. Then he remembered the others were listening and watching him lose his cool. At least the communication was only one-way.

"Monitor the GPS tracker and get your tails over here ASAP. We'll trade vehicles."

They could also swap the license plates. No doubt Dean had taken note of the tags.

There was only one compact spare in the trunk. A doughnut. Dean had flattened two tires. They'd need the spares from both vehicles.

He popped the trunk and pulled out the jack and spare. Might as well get started. He didn't want those mercs thinking he was above menial labor and intended to rest on his laurels waiting for them to do it. Messing up with Dean in the nursing home was his first mistake. He wouldn't be allowed a second.

His phone buzzed. He took it out and looked at the screen. *Ava.*

It was the team calling him. Butch had suggested he save whatever contact number the team gave him under a woman's name. In the event Dean considered trusting him, he would check Lucas's phone and search his call history. Easy to explain a girlfriend checking in. Multiple calls could be dismissed as relationship issues, yada, yada.

He answered. "What's up? Is there a problem?"

"The target is headed back in your direction."

"What?" Lucas glanced at the road.

"ETA to your location two minutes."

That was unexpected. What could've possibly possessed Dean to turn around?

"Got it. Keep your distance. One to two miles back. If he gets a whiff of you, senses you near, this won't work."

"Roger."

Lucas put his phone away.

Quickly, he plotted his next move and the one thereafter and determined what he needed to do. He opened the back door and grabbed the contingency kit. Inside he looked over the various items and decided to take only one.

It was small, and if Dean searched him, he wouldn't find it.

He slipped it deep in his pocket and stowed the kit under the front seat.

Then he grabbed the tire iron, removed the hubcap and started loosening the lug nuts.

Lucas sensed Dean drawing closer before he saw his Jeep Renegade. Glancing over his shoulder, he met Dean's wary gaze. No mask this time. The vehicle inched up slowly. Dean's head was on a swivel as if still waiting for others to appear.

"Are you really here on your own?" Dean asked.

"I am, Santa. If I was with a team, I'd have a little help with this." Lucas gestured to one of the flats and stood. "What brings you back here?"

Dean clenched his jaw. "Hell has frozen over. I need your help."

Chapter Sixteen

Cold water splashed onto Kate's face ripped her from unconsciousness. Snorting some up her nose, she coughed. She went to push the wet hair from her face to discover that she couldn't move. She was tied to a chair in the middle of a large, open dusty space.

In front of her, Jim sat in a folding chair, watching her.

Little by little memories came back to her. Being in the car with Jim. The questions. The sweet smell.

A guy came over to Jim, and that's when she saw the other men. Five more. Armed with guns. They all had the same rough, edgy look to them.

"The truck is loaded," the man said.

"Get the product moving. I want the distro done today." Jim glanced at his watch. "Let the others know that once I make the call and give Dean the location, they need to stay vigilant. That one is crafty."

"Yes, sir." He flounced off back to the others.

"Dean?" she asked, her brain still a bit foggy.

Jim got up, grabbed a handful of paper towels from a table and wiped her face gently, as if he actually cared about her welfare.

She shrank back from his touch, knowing nothing could be farther from the truth.

"Yes. I pieced together that DJ is Dean Delgado."

"How? When?"

Jim sat back in the chair facing her and crossed his legs. "Well, the other night when he took down my two guys who went after Cheryl, the first red flag popped up. DJ is supposed to be going on eighty, and he bested young, virile men with little to no injury to himself. Then you said his name, Dean, when I phoned you. Another red flag. You came to my office yesterday wearing a man's sweater, spouting off some cockamamie story about a Good Samaritan. In your haste to leave, you forgot the gloves. A pair of men's gloves. I went after you to give them back and overheard your conversation with Janeen. I watched you walk down to the *Gazette*. Saw *DJ* waltz in shortly thereafter. The two of you left with a folder, looking thick as thieves. Then I called you. Asked you if you'd seen him or had a working phone number for him."

A sinking feeling washed through her, from her head to her toes. If she'd been standing, she would've swayed on her feet from the sickening rush of it.

"You were with him. Lying to me. So naturally, I had to wonder why a good girl like Katie Sawyer, who had never lied to me before, was suddenly pathological in her attempts to safeguard her friendly neighborhood bartender."

Kate dry heaved, wanting to retch, but nothing came up.

"Then I recalled how eighty-year-old DJ gave chase after Smitty. Witnessed the car accident. So, I checked the CCTV footage from that night. Lo and behold, who did I see? Everything *almost* made sense. It took me a little bit to figure out why he's been traipsing around town, for months, in disguise." Jim tapped his temple. "Because Dean is in some kind of trouble. He's running from something or someone. And that's why you and lover boy were planning to leave town together."

"We'll disappear. We won't say anything to anybody. You'll never see us again. We won't be a problem."

"You're absolutely right. After you're both dead and buried, that'll be two less problems to worry about."

Oh, God! Oh, God! He was going to kill them.

"I didn't want it to come to this, Katie. After Cheryl died, I checked her belongings for the thumb drive before I left the hospital. When I sent one of my guys to your place to see if you had it, I gave strict instructions not to kill you. I was so pleased when you ended up bringing it to me. But then you lied to me over and over again. You brought this on yourself."

"You murdered Tyler, didn't you?"

He cocked his head to the side. "I gave the order. One of my boys carried it out."

Her chest tightened as if caught in a vise, her mind racing over everything Jim had said. "Andrea. Please don't hurt her. She won't talk."

"She was warned. She didn't heed it."

"You don't have to kill her."

"Andrea Miles is dead. She died this morning. Slipped in the shower. Broke her neck. Unfortunate freak accident. They haven't found her body yet. But they will soon."

Kate shook her head, fighting the rising panic. "What about the baby? Are you going to kill him, too?" Where did the trail of bloodshed and horror end?

"Do you think I'm a monster?" He reeled back in his chair with a look of disgust. "I wouldn't hurt an innocent baby."

"You never even got the paternity test done, did you?"

"I definitely did." He nodded. "My guys aren't the father, but I already knew that. I was just looking for confirmation that the kid is the governor's son. That boy is going to give me all the leverage I'll ever need against him. The governor has aspirations to run for president one day." Jim whistled. "It's going to be nice having the power of the White House at my beck and call. An ace up my sleeve that he won't see coming. That chump doesn't even know the baby has been born. Cheryl wasn't due until next month."

"Why are you doing this? Drugs? Forced prostitution?" To think she had once admired this man.

"Money and power. I can't afford an Ivy League tuition on a public servant's salary. I'm up for reelection this year. Campaigning and billboards cost money. This operation funded the governor's campaign as well. He picked a circuit judge who owed him a favor, so we could get the right girls for this enterprise. We have a lucrative side hustle, a good thing going."

"It's not good for the women you force into this. Is Holden a part of this, too?"

"Holden?" Jim snickered. "That Boy Scout. Heck, no."

"But Renee…"

"I encouraged Renee to sidle up to him. So I could keep an eye on him. Make sure he doesn't go sticking his nose where it doesn't belong. I like him. A good deputy. I'd hate to have to kill him." His watch beeped. "Almost time to call lover boy."

"TELL ME AGAIN," Dean said to Lucas, wishing he could torture him to get honest answers. It was his operational instincts talking. Torture would only alienate his brother, and he didn't want to hurt Lucas. But the method was effective at getting the truth.

"How many times are we going to go over this?"

"As many as necessary." Asking the same questions over and over, making a person repeat their story, exposed cracks in the lies. But Dean was aware that Lucas was just as highly trained as he was, which would make it difficult to distinguish between lies and the truth.

This was a drill Lucas was familiar with. A game he played well.

Hands clenched on the steering wheel as he drove them to Nelson's Gun and Outdoor Sports shop, Dean said, "I'm waiting."

Lucas sighed. "Butch was waiting for me when I stepped off the elevator."

"He didn't call you in early?"

"No. He ambushed me. Hauled me into Price's office. Clark was seated. Your old handler Russell was standing. They said you had been caught on CCTV in our hometown. They were putting a team together and wanted me to give them any information to help track you down."

"What did you tell them?"

"Everything," Lucas said bluntly. Quite convincingly. "About mom, her Alzheimer's. I explained that you wouldn't go creeping back to Laramie for *her*, though."

Dean tensed, hating the grain of truth in that. If Kate hadn't still been living here, he probably would've chosen a different location.

"I told them to look for Kate."

"Every time you say that, it makes me want to wring your neck."

"It shouldn't. I came here to intervene. To find you. To make sure those mercs never laid a finger on Kate. And I'm here, right? In this car with you, ready to risk my life to rescue her from the sheriff. Why? Because I care about her, too. She means a lot to me. I wouldn't have made it out of this town alive without her."

A flicker of something darted across his face, so fast if Dean had blinked, he would've missed it. *Pain.*

The pain his brother felt was deep and genuine.

But was it deep enough to poison Lucas, turn him into a backstabbing liar out for revenge?

That was the question he still hadn't answered.

Dean pulled up in front of Nelson's. "Only purchase the items we discussed, and pay in cash."

Lucas rolled his eyes. "I'm not an amateur. This isn't my first rodeo." He pulled the handle, opening the door.

"Hang on," Dean said. "Give me your phone."

"What for? You still don't trust me?"

"Trust has to be earned. One baby step at a time." Dean held out his palm. "Phone."

Lucas took out his cell, entered the pass code and dropped it into his hand.

For good measure, Dean felt his jacket pockets and pulled up his pant legs, taking a gander at his ankles, to be sure he didn't have a second phone hidden on him.

"Satisfied?" Lucas asked.

"Not even close. Hurry up. The call will be coming soon."

Lucas jumped out and went into the shop.

As much as he wanted to believe that his little brother was willing to set aside his grievances and had come

here to help him, something in his gut simply wouldn't
let him.

He only trusted him enough to partner up to save
Kate.

Dean swiped across the screen of the phone and
searched his recent call history.

Missed calls from a Langley number. Even more
missed calls from Butch, his team leader. Which would
make sense if Lucas had left work and hopped on a plane
as he had claimed.

The only call he'd taken in the last twenty-four hours
was from Ava. Probably a girlfriend.

Dean glanced in the back seat at Lucas's duffel bag.
Unzipping it, he riffled through his things, searching
for anything suspect. No gun. No ammo. He wouldn't
have been able to fly commercial with one. That made
sense, too.

*If it looks like a duck and quacks like a duck, it's a
duck, right?*

Then why did he feel as if he was playing a game of
Duck, Duck, Goose instead? One where Lucas was going
to turn out to be a spiteful goose.

The CIA was the best at this, painting any picture
they wanted you to see while hiding the truth.

It didn't help matters that even as a kid, if someone
wronged Lucas, he never let it go.

Dean swiped the screen again. This time he checked
his text messages. Not a single one from *Ava*. No calls
from her last week, either.

He blew out a heavy breath. That didn't prove anything. Ava could be someone new. A girl he just met.

Dean's cell phone rang. His heart pounded as he answered. "Yes."

"Do you have what you stole from me?"

"Yes."

"Come to the old cement plant on the south side of town. Do you know the one?"

Did he ever. The perfect spot to meet. Isolated. No one would hear gunfire. Plenty of places for armed men to hide. "Yes."

"Be here in twenty minutes, or she dies." Jim hung up.

Dean's gut burned. He ached to put Sheriff Jim Ames down. Six feet under with one bullet to the head.

Lucas pushed through the door of the shop and came back to the car, holding a bag of guns, ammo and a big black case with the words *Electric Fire Remote Ignition System* printed across the front.

"The call came," Dean said as his brother got settled in his seat.

"Where do we meet?"

He handed Lucas his cell phone. "The old cement plant."

"Good choice on the sheriff's part. You definitely need me."

That was true.

Lucas passed him the shopping bag. "You load while I set these puppies up." He patted the case.

Inside the bag were two tactical nine-millimeters. Both used, probably to keep the costs down. Threaded barrels. Nelson's didn't sell silencers. Dean would loan Lucas his sound suppressor, but his brother wasn't touching his personal weapon.

Not that Dean would be able to bring it with him inside the cement plant. He fully expected to be searched and for any weapons found to be confiscated.

While Dean loaded the guns for Lucas, his brother

took out the sport smoke canisters and programmed them to go off with the remote control. Lucas would search for the men who were lying in wait and eliminate them. Along the way, he'd leave behind a smoke canister.

When Dean gave him the signal, Lucas would ignite them with a press of a button.

"Once you're inside the plant, you'll need to be fast and quiet. We have to get Kate out of there and to safety."

Lucas took the gun with attached sound suppressor. Checked that it was loaded and chambered a round. "I know how to do a job."

His brother had a reputation for being one of the best in-house assassins.

But once you were trained and had enough ops under your belt, the hard part wasn't killing. It was not losing your humanity in the process.

Dean didn't doubt that Lucas would be able to take out a bunch of thugs.

He worried that the man beside him might not be his brother anymore.

Chapter Seventeen

Dean had looped around to the back of the plant and stopped the Jeep.

Lucas hopped out with the gear he needed. Standing between the car and the open door, he stared at Dean. "Do me a favor?"

"What's that?"

Lucas pointed the gun at Dean's head. His finger was on the trigger. If Lucas had still been in the car, in close proximity, he could've taken him. But with his brother out of the car with a clear, clean shot, Dean didn't stand a chance.

"Once the dust settles," Lucas said, "I want you to look back on this moment and remember that I had a choice." He lowered the gun, shut the door and gave him a two-finger salute.

Dean let out the breath that he'd been holding. For the longest heartbeat, he hadn't been sure if Lucas would've pulled the trigger.

After watching his brother sneak into the plant, using the entrance he'd indicated, Dean took out his cell phone and tapped the iHere app, activating it. He'd downloaded the app ages ago, and it was paired with a triangular device, smaller than a key fob, that was attached to his key chain. He put the cell phone to sleep. When he was ready, with a push of the button on the device, he could secretly begin recording a conversation. The phone would appear as if still in sleep mode, but every word would be captured.

If he was lucky, the sheriff would be feeling cocky, emboldened to say more than he should.

Dean drove around to the front and parked. He leaned over and took out a flip phone, a burner, from the glove box. Getting out of the car, he scanned his surroundings.

One guy was waiting for him by a door. "Where are the girls?" he asked as Dean approached.

"That's a conversation for me to have with your boss." He extended his arms in preparation to be searched, the keys with the iHere device in his right hand and the flip phone in his left.

The guard did a quick pat down of his arms, torso and legs, pausing to take a look at the cell phone in his pocket. It never occurred to the obtuse man to ask why Dean had two phones. Noticing that the smartphone was asleep, the guy stuffed it back in Dean's pocket.

The guy turned a gun on Dean, and they walked through the cement plant to the large, open area where he'd witnessed them loading drugs the last time he'd been there.

Kate was standing beside a chair with her wrists bound. The sheriff was beside her, gun in his hand pointed at her.

Seeing panic race across her face almost did Dean in. A killing rage spiked through him, and that red haze clouding everything thickened.

"Dean Delgado, as I live and breathe."

Not for much longer, if Dean had anything to say

about it. He pressed the button, activating the recording app. "Kate, are you okay?"

She teared up and pressed her lips tight like she'd been instructed not to speak.

The sheriff grabbed her by the arm. "Don't talk to her. Talk to me. Where are the girls?"

"Do you think I was stupid enough to bring them here? They're somewhere safe."

"Now that was a mistake." The sheriff pressed the muzzle of his gun into Kate's ribs, and she winced.

The look of pure fear in her eyes hit Dean straight in the gut. Jim Ames was going to die today.

"The mistake would be killing Kate, Sheriff. I may not have those poor women you forced into prostitution, innocent girls—"

"They weren't innocent." An ugly grin spread across his face. "According to the law, they were all found guilty as charged. If they had been good girls, keeping their noses clean, doing the right thing, then they would be innocent."

This hubris would be the sheriff's downfall. He was used to controlling everything and everyone. Thought himself above the law. Had grown to think he was invincible.

"You had the parole officer Renee Olson intimidate and coerce them," Dean said, stalling to give Lucas time to work and hopefully to get something that would strengthen the FBI's case. "I assume the judge must be getting paid off, too, sentencing them to that halfway house."

"Sure, the governor's second circuit man gets a kickback."

"It's disgusting. Pumping those women full of drugs, using them like pieces of meat."

"We've all got to make a living. Those girls don't bring in nearly as much money as the drugs, but it's a nice slice of the pie that I'm not willing to give up. You have until the count of three to tell me where my cash cows are, or I put a bullet in her. One."

"Don't tell him," Kate said. "He's going to kill us anyway."

The sheriff raised his hand and hit Kate with the gun he held—a quick, startling smack to her cheek. She cried out as blood dribbled from her mouth, and then she held her face.

Dean took a step forward, but the other man, a punk with a gun, pressed the muzzle to the right side of his head. The proximity was excellent. Just right for Dean to maneuver when the time came.

"I warned you, Katie." The sheriff hit her again. This time in her stomach, and she doubled over, crumpling to her knees. "Shut your mouth."

The breath stalled in Dean's lungs, and his knees went weak. The sheriff was a sick, evil man, but Dean hadn't been prepared for him to strike her. To hit her with such brutal force. "Don't you dare touch her again."

Jim stared him in the eyes as he grabbed a handful of Kate's hair and yanked her up to her feet. "Two."

"I'll give you two reasons you're not killing anyone today," Dean said. "First, this phone in my hand is a remote detonator. I hit the send button, the number is called and one of your distro sites along with a whole lot of crystal meth goes *boom*."

Jim's eyes narrowed. "You're lying."

He was. This was a total bluff.

Dean rattled off the coordinates of the other location he visited. "The one near Rock River. I planted quite a bit of BLASTEX," he said, referring to the brand of packaged explosives used by construction workers. And that was true. He had planted explosives somewhere. Months ago. But it wasn't at one of the drug sites. "My fake demolitions credentials came in handy."

"I could just have him shoot you." Jim gestured to the guy holding the gun on Dean.

"My finger will hit the button before he pulls the trigger, but if he kills me, you'll never find those women. Which brings me to my second reason. I'm not here alone. Now!"

The Electric Fire canisters detonated, emitting huge bursts of white smoke in various spots where Lucas had placed them. A perfect distraction that drew the sheriff's and the other man's attention, their heads swiveling, their gazes flying around wildly.

Dean moved lightning fast. He dropped his keys as he cocked his arm, swinging his elbow back and rotating his body. The pointy bone collided with the man's head and sent him reeling. Seizing the momentum, Dean struck the guy's arm. Then he twisted the weapon loose from his grip and fired two shots at his chest.

With the gun in hand, Dean whirled and took aim on the sheriff, but Jim had his arm wrapped around Kate's throat, holding her in front of him as a human shield.

No matter what, this was ending here, with Jim Ames in a pool of his own blood. "You're the one dying today," Dean vowed. "Let her go."

Jim laughed, so arrogant, so sure of himself. He had no idea whom he was dealing with.

In his peripheral vision, Dean saw Lucas emerge from

the smoke, holding the sound-suppressed nine-millimeter at the ready.

He gave a little nod of thanks to his brother, and both men trained their weapons on the sheriff.

Jim had missed this one important fact. His skills were nothing up against theirs, those of trained killers, molded by the CIA. The sheriff's greed paled in comparison to Dean's fear for Kate and his determination to keep her safe, even at the cost of his life.

"You won't shoot me." Jim tightened his hold on Kate. "Not while I have her."

"Dean," Kate muttered.

His gaze fell to her terrified face. *Please, don't talk, honey.* He needed to focus. Couldn't afford the distraction of looking at her, hearing her.

Lucas glanced between them. He must have had some idea of how this was messing with Dean's head, because he spoke up. "Kate, let us do what we do best. Just be quiet."

But Kate kept her gaze focused on Dean's. The intensity of it burned through him. "It's okay." Her bloody lip trembled. "Do it."

He shook his head. "What?" She couldn't possibly mean…

"You have to stop him." A tear ran down her cheek.

Jim tightened his arm around her throat, choking her, and it was as if someone had knifed Dean and ripped him open. He couldn't lose her, and he couldn't risk her life by taking a dodgy shot that wasn't clean.

"I'm walking out of here." Jim shook her as he dragged her along with him, creeping toward an exit. "And you're going to let me leave if you want her to live."

Kate struggled against him, trying to pry his arm

from her throat. "I love you." Her voice was raspy, the words crashing together. "Kill him. Take the shot."

Dean's vision blurred. *No, not like this.* He couldn't take the shot with the gun pointed to her head.

"Rotten bastard! I never liked you," Lucas said. "I called 911 and you didn't arrest him. I was bloody and beaten. My mom was bloody. And you didn't arrest him!" Lucas charged the sheriff.

Jim swung his gun away from Kate toward Lucas, giving Dean the opportunity. The opening. He took the shot.

The force of the bullet knocked Jim Ames backward, but the arm locked around Kate hauled her down to the floor with him.

Dean and Lucas rushed to her. His brother pried the arm loose from her throat. Dean hauled her up into his arms. He ran a hand over her hair and face. Fear released the icy grip it had on his heart.

She was shaking. Her cheek was bruised. Her abdomen must've hurt as well. There was blood in her hair and dust all over her clothes.

The dazed expression didn't clear from her eyes and probably wouldn't for a while.

But she was alive.

Unlike the sheriff, who was dead with blood pooling around his head.

"We should get out of here," Lucas said, scooping up Dean's car keys.

Dean gave a nod. "Let's go."

With Dean on one side of Kate and Lucas on the other, they got her to the car. Lucas tossed him the keys. Dean put her in the back where she could lie down with Lucas's bag under her head.

"Give them to me." Dean held out his hand to his brother and waited for him to pass over the guns.

"After that, you still don't trust me?"

"Lunging at Ames wasn't about me or Kate, that was about you." Getting revenge and not letting go of anything from the past.

Lucas put the two guns in Dean's hands.

Dean dropped them in the foot well beneath him, did a quick pat down on Lucas to be sure he didn't have others from the men he'd killed and took off. He sped toward the motel and didn't slow until they had arrived. "Help me get her into the room."

Lucas gave a slight nod.

They got Kate out of the car into the motel room.

"Smells like sex and stale coffee in here," Lucas said.

Dean grimaced at him. "Shut up."

They sat Kate down on the bed.

"Hon, are you all right?" Dean asked. She nodded but didn't say anything, and that's what worried him. "I'm going to get some ice for her face." Dean jumped up, grabbing the plastic bag from the ice bucket and darted out of the room.

He ran to the ice machine. Put the bag under the opening of the chute and slapped the button. Once the bag was full of ice, he dashed back to the room, swiped the key card and rushed inside.

Kate was saying something low to Lucas. His arm was around her, and her head was resting on his shoulder. An inkling of jealousy twisted through him, but his relief at seeing her come out of that trance and responding was worth so much more.

Lucas looked up at him. "Dean loves you so much he actually let me help."

"Thank you," she said to Lucas. "For coming. For helping us."

"That's what family is for." Lucas rubbed her arm, holding her close.

Dean stepped up to Kate and handed her the bag of ice. "Put this on your face. The sheriff hit you pretty hard."

"Thanks." She took the bag with one hand and clutched his wrist with the other. "I know how much you risked by coming for me."

"I'm nothing without you." That was the extent of what he could say, confess, in front of his brother. "Put the ice on your face."

She did and winced.

Tomorrow, she'd thank him for it.

Dean went to the laptop on the nightstand and got to work. First, he connected his phone and began the download of the recorded conversation. He dug in his bag and found a spare thumb drive. After he erased anything on it, he copied all the pertinent files for the FBI, including the recording from earlier today of the sheriff at the cement plant.

Taking the drive from the computer, he turned to his brother. "Why are you here?"

Lucas's gaze lifted from Kate to his. "Isn't that obvious by now?"

No, it wasn't. "What was the first thing you felt when you saw Butch in the vault and he told you he'd been waiting for you?"

"I was in the elevator when I saw Butch that morning. And the first thing I felt was surprised."

Dean believed that when Butch had approached him it had been in the elevator.

"Who was in Price's office?" he asked, stepping closer, wanting to hear the story again.

"Clark was seated in a chair. Kelly Russell was standing beside Price. At his right hand."

Details were important, especially if you were lying. But this hadn't changed. The positioning of the players.

But this time around Dean homed in on something he'd missed before. "I get why they might call her in for this meeting, but why was the ice queen standing next to Price? Why wasn't she sitting when you came in?"

Lucas got up and walked over to Dean. "I forgot to tell you the best part. Russell was promoted after your disastrous operation that made you all traitors."

"What?" Dean stared at Lucas, horrified, disgusted. "She didn't get fired or quit in outrage over the injustice of what happened?"

"No, they didn't fire her, and she most certainly didn't quit." Lucas said the words plainly, matter-of-factly. "She was promoted to deputy director of operations, and she's gunning for Topaz."

If that was true, then either Kelly Russell had set them up on that ruinous mission and she wanted to tie up loose ends, or... "She believes we're traitors. She doesn't question our guilt?"

"Everyone believes you're guilty."

"Why?"

"Because of the money."

"What money?"

Something shifted in his brother's eyes. "The offshore accounts with your names on it. Half a million dollars each."

This was bad. Worse than he'd imagined.

"The ice queen spearheaded this operation to hunt

you down, Dean. She was the one who wanted me to give them information about you."

And that's where his dear little brother had given him too much truth.

Lucas had almost convinced him that he was there out of brotherly concern.

No one was better than Kelly Russell at reading people, sizing them up, measuring their strengths, assessing their weaknesses.

Maybe Russell had let Lucas waltz out of Langley in the middle of the day after questioning him, let him come here and had him followed, had a tracker put on him.

But then a kill team would have taken Dean out by now.

Maybe Russell had sent Lucas for some other reason.

Either way, Lucas wasn't a duck. His brother was a big, fat, golden goose.

"I have to run an errand," Dean said. "Mail some information, overnight express it to someone. I'll be back in a little while."

"I can go to the post office for you," Lucas offered. "It's best you don't flash your face around town with a kill team hunting you."

Dean put a ball cap on his head. "Your concern warms my heart, but I'll take care of it myself. You stay here." He grabbed the thumb drive with all the data, the hard-copy folder from Andrea and his personal duffel bag with all his stuff. No way he was leaving any of his gear within his brother's reach. He kissed Kate's forehead. "Keep the ice on your face," he said to her, "and an eye on him." He gestured to his brother. "Don't let him out of your sight."

Chapter Eighteen

Kate watched Dean waltz out of the motel room with all his belongings, and for a startling heartbeat, she wondered if he was coming back.

He loves you. He won't leave you again.

"Kate." Lucas held one of her hands in his. "I'm so glad you're okay. Safe."

She pressed the ice to her cheek, where the sheriff had hit her. "I'm just glad you were there to help us. When I saw Dean walk in, I was so scared for him. I knew Jim had four other men hiding, waiting to kill him." She squeezed her fingers around his. "What are you doing here?"

"The CIA tried to recruit me to help track down Dean. But when I heard he was in Laramie, I knew he was here because of you."

"You did?"

"There's no other reason he would've come back here."

Pride and her ego swelled for moment, then Kate thought of his mother. "Did the CIA ask you to come?"

"No." Lucas shook his head, holding her gaze. "In fact, I'm going to get into a lot of trouble for coming here. If they don't fire me, they'll probably send a kill team after me, too."

"Oh, no."

"But I had to help him and to protect you. I inadvertently told them about your relationship as teenagers. When I did, I saw it in their eyes, that they considered you to be a viable target he'd make contact with. I couldn't let anything happen to you because I'd slipped up."

"Lucas, you've risked so much."

"I never thought I would. Not in a million years. Not for him. Not after he abandoned us." The crestfallen look on his face broke her heart.

She recalled far too vividly the grief-stricken, angry boy he'd been. His grades at school had nosedived; he constantly got into fights and was a regular in detention. Until she helped him. Studied with him. Invited him to her house for dinners to give him a break. Did her best to fill the hole Dean had left behind.

"He regrets it," she said. "He's sorry for leaving the way he did. It wasn't to hurt us."

"But it did hurt us. Both of us. Do you know he's never apologized to me?"

"He said you won't talk to him. That he's tried."

"He's a liar." Lucas got up, took off his jacket and tossed it on the dresser. "He hasn't tried. Dean saw me once in the hall, and when I blew him off, the way he deserved, do you know what he did?"

She set the ice down. "What?"

"Nothing. Not a thing. I'm his brother, not only in blood, but in the Corps, too, a bond that's supposed to be unbreakable. That transcends blood. A lot of good it's done me."

"You joined the marines, too? How did you know he joined the Corps?"

"Mom received a letter congratulating her on his completion of basic training," he said.

Kate knew his mother had burned the letter, but she didn't know she'd shown it to Lucas.

"She cried. She was so happy to know that he was alive and okay. Not dead on the street." He clenched his jaw. "If Dean was really sorry, if he cared about me at all, he would've tried every day. He never would've stopped trying until I forgave him. But here I am, like a fool. I'm the one trying to help him. He doesn't even appreciate it. Treating me like I'm the enemy instead of giving me a chance when I'm the one who's done nothing wrong."

He was still so angry, so hurt.

"Lucas." She got up and embraced him.

"I've risked everything, and he's just going to leave me behind. Again."

"No." Kate pulled back and looked at him. "He won't. I won't let him."

"He doesn't care about me." The pain in his eyes, in his voice, tore her apart.

"That's not true. He loves you. I'll talk to him. You'll see." Dean needed to mend this fence with his brother. It was his responsibility. He was the one who left; he was the oldest. Dean had to make this right.

"What would I do without you, Kate?"

She smiled, but the searing pain was too much.

Lucas put a gentle hand on her shoulder. "I'm so sorry the sheriff hurt you."

"At least he's dead now." Thank goodness for that.

Lucas looked her over. "You're a mess. There's blood

in your hair and you're covered in dust. Do you want to clean up?"

"Yeah, actually, I do." Her muscles loosened at the thought of a warm shower. She headed for the bathroom. "I'll only be five minutes."

"Take your time. I'll watch something on TV."

DEAN DISCONNECTED THE call after talking with his cousin Lourdes, who was there in Laramie. Lola wasn't going to open the bar today and would head straight to Fort Collins. It would have been faster to simply hand her all the evidence he had for the FBI so that she could give it to her brother, but a kill team would most certainly have her under surveillance.

Hopping out of the Jeep, he walked into the post office and sent everything overnight express. Back at his vehicle, he grabbed his bag of gear and took out a device that looked like a black wand. He toggled the switch, turning it on. Then he swept his vehicle for a tracking device.

It didn't take long for the wand to beep.

Bingo.

Well, that answered his question about whether or not Russell had had Lucas followed or had sent him.

Dean had to hand it to the ice queen. Her plan was pretty brilliant. But what was she after? Why wasn't he already dead?

Leaving the tracking device undisturbed, he stowed the wand back in the bag and dug around until he found what he was searching for. It looked like an EpiPen, but it was loaded with ketamine instead of epinephrine. He slipped it in his pocket, closed the door and crossed the street.

Keeping his head lowered, he walked one more block.

Driving would have been faster, but he didn't want whoever was monitoring the tracker on his vehicle to know where he was going.

He strolled into Nelson's, the same gun shop he'd stopped at earlier, and went up to the counter. "I'd like to get a box of blank nine-millimeter cartridges."

WITH A TOWEL wrapped around her body, Kate finished blow-drying her hair. She ran a brush through it, feeling more like herself. The last couple of days had been the toughest in her life, and the best.

Because she had Dean.

And now it was up to her make sure the Delgado brothers made amends. They'd been estranged far too long.

Looking around, she realized she'd forgotten to bring in a fresh change of clothes with her. She opened the bathroom door, and Lucas was standing there, fist raised like he was about to knock.

"Here you go." He handed her some clothes, neatly folded.

"You must be a mind reader."

He smiled, bright and warm. Both he and his brother were tall and handsome, Dean in a sexier, rugged way, but Lucas was so darned cute with those dimples.

"Just observant," he said. "You didn't take any in with you."

"Thanks."

She shut the door. He'd chosen jeans and a sweater. Not that she had a lot of options in the bag. Putting on her underwear, she flushed at the thought of Lucas touching her unmentionables, but it was sweet of him to get her clothes.

Kate left the bathroom, dressed, and packed up her things. When Dean got back, they'd probably head straight out.

Lucas was in a chair watching a show on the home and garden channel about a house renovation.

She heard a vehicle pull up and glanced out the window. Dean was back. She put on her coat, zipped it and grabbed her bag. "I'm going to talk to him."

"He won't listen to reason, because I mean nothing to him."

"You're his brother, and he loves you. I'll make him listen."

Kate stepped outside and shut the door just as Dean reached it. She dropped her bag.

"What are you doing out here?" he asked.

"We need to talk."

"You should be in there watching him," he snapped, pointing a finger at the room.

"He doesn't need to be watched. He's not a criminal."

Dean rolled his eyes and tipped his head back. "You've got to be kidding me."

She grabbed his arm and tugged him two doors down. "I can't believe you."

"Me? What did I do wrong?"

Oh, let her count the ways. "You ran into your brother after not seeing him for a decade and a half and only spoke to him once."

"He wouldn't talk to me."

"He's angry. He's hurt. And it's all justified. You were in the wrong." She stabbed his chest with a finger. "You should have gone to his apartment. Stopped by his desk at work. You should have tried to make things right with him every single day. But you didn't. How do you think that made him feel? Huh?"

"Damn it, he got to you."

She recoiled. "Got to me? Do you have a heart in there?" She stabbed his chest again.

Dean lowered his head. "You're right. I should have done better. I could have done more."

"You should have gotten down on your knees and begged for his forgiveness. You have no idea how hard it was for him without you."

"I'm not the bad guy here."

"Neither is he."

"Oh, yes, he is."

"Stop." She raised her palm. "I won't listen to you say one bad thing about him. Do you understand me? After he left Laramie, did he forget about you? Forge his own path? No. He joined the Marine Corps and the CIA. Why do you think that is, Dean? He's been following you, hoping that you'd care enough to notice. He is your little brother. And he's going to come with us."

"No." Dean stepped back. "No, he's not. You don't understand—"

"If he doesn't go, I don't go. I love you and want nothing more than to be with you, but this is where I draw the line." She turned on her heel.

He ran around in front of her, stopping her.

"I mean it, Dean Delgado. There's *nothing* you can say that will make me change my mind."

"I believe you."

She rocked back, not expecting that response.

"We will leave this motel together, but you have to promise to do two things for me."

It had better not have anything to do with leaving Lucas. She would not agree to it. "What?"

"If I ever use the word *Heathcliff*, you are to move away from me and him and take cover."

Her heart seized. "Why?"

"Do you agree?"

She hesitated. "Yes," she said uneasily. "What's the second thing?"

He handed her an EpiPen.

"What's this for? You don't have allergies."

"You hold on to it. Put it in your coat pocket," he said, and she did. "When I ask you for it, you give it to me."

Her nerves stretched taut. Something was going on, something important was happening in this moment, but she didn't understand what. "Is that it?"

"That's it."

"He goes with us?"

"We're all getting in the car together."

She reached up and threaded her arms around his neck, her heart so full she was sure her chest couldn't contain it. "Thank you." She kissed him, lightly, tenderly since her face still ached. "I love you."

"I love you, too. I'm doing this for you."

Pulling back, she stared at him. "You should be doing this for yourself and for him. Not for me."

"Still. This is all for you."

Chapter Nineteen

"Here you go." Dean reached toward the back seat and handed Lucas the two guns he'd purchased.

"So, does this mean you finally trust me?" Lucas asked.

Not a snowball's chance in hell. "I have to at some point, right?"

Lucas smiled, putting one gun in his coat pocket and the other in his bag.

Kate put her hand on Dean's leg and rubbed his thigh, her eyes gleaming with approval.

Dean pulled out of the motel parking lot and drove to Route 287, taking it south. Everything that Kate had said weighed on him. Lucas wasn't a bad person. He was a good guy, twisted by pain and rage, misled by the CIA. Dean realized Lucas had never asked for his side of the story, his version of events that had gotten him branded a traitor.

Everyone believes you're guilty.

That included Lucas, and that was Dean's fault.

If he had done all the things that Kate had suggested, proven to Lucas that he was sorry, made a halfway-decent effort to reconnect, then his little brother wouldn't be in the back seat of the Jeep, feeling justified about betraying him.

This was a powder keg of Dean's own making.

"Where are we heading?" Lucas asked.

Dean checked his rearview mirror. The kill team was out there, following them, but at such a distance, he couldn't spot them. No need for them to keep a visual. Not when there was a tracker on the vehicle. "Someplace safe. It's a short drive."

"Short?" Lucas leaned forward. "We need to get out of the state."

"We are."

But not with him.

First, he had to show Kate that the divide between him and his brother was too great to bridge in a day. It was the freaking Grand Canyon.

Even if he had told her about the tracker on the car, she would've wanted to discuss it with Lucas, give him a chance to explain.

There was only one way to resolve this so that she left with him. Didn't hate him for not taking Lucas along.

Dean drove to The Buttes. A small unincorporated community that had a population of about fifty. Once there, he took an unmarked dirt road to an old airfield he'd scoped out after he'd returned.

"We're flying out?" Lucas asked.

No, they weren't. "Yep." Dean pointed to the dilapidated aircraft hangar that was about four times the size of a garage. Attached to it was a small office building with a few busted-out windows.

He stopped the car a good 150 feet back and to the side of the hangar.

They all got out, grabbing their bags. Dean unlocked

the padlock he'd put on the hangar door, and the hinges creaked with a loud groan when he opened it.

Kate and Lucas followed him inside.

There was a broken-down twin prop plane in the hangar. He'd salvaged parts for the exterior and painted them to make the aircraft appear functional. Nothing more than a shell with a hollow interior that he had packed with some BLASTEX. The preprogrammed number in the flip phone in his pocket would trigger the detonator.

This was his contingency plan. Every good operative had one.

"See, I told you this would work out," Kate said to Lucas.

"Yeah, you were right. I never doubted you."

Dean set his bag on an old, dusty desk, keeping his back to them.

"What's our destination?" Lucas asked.

"Someplace warm," Dean said.

"Wouldn't you like to know, Kate?" Lucas prodded.

"Actually, I would." Her voice was light and so carefree.

That was about to change.

"Come on, Dean. If you really trusted me, you'd tell me. Are we going to meet up with the rest of your team?"

There it is. The reason Kelly Russell had sent Lucas. The reason Dean was still breathing. They thought he would lead them to the rest of his team.

He didn't know where any of them were. But he did have a way to contact Hunter, his team leader. Hunter had given them each a satellite phone. One programmed number. Their last-resort measure if they had nowhere else to go.

Only Hunter would answer the line. Then there would be a challenge and response. Hunter would say *parachute*. Dean would have to respond with *rip cord*, and he'd be given instructions and coordinates to Hunter's location.

And that's what the ice queen was counting on. She knew Hunter well. That their team was a family. That Hunter would never leave any of them hanging, blowing in the wind. That he'd given them a way to contact him.

"As a matter of fact, we are," Dean said, facing his brother. "I hope you have a passport that the agency can't track. I've got ones for Kate and me. From here on out, she's going to be Emily and I'm going to be Heathcliff."

Kate's smile fell, and she stiffened.

Dean shot her a hard look. Things were going to get physical with his brother, and he didn't want her accidentally getting hurt because she was standing too close. "I know *Heathcliff* is a mouthful. You can call me Cliff for short if you like."

She glanced between them and slowly backed away toward the plane.

"No worries on the passport for me," Lucas said, focused on Dean and pumping him for information. "So, where are we going?"

Without answering, Dean turned back around to his bag and unzipped it. He stared down at his spare gun, the backup, that was resting on top of his clothes beside the black wand.

"I think I've proven I can be trusted," Lucas said.

"Panama," Dean said, picking someplace he'd been to once on vacation. "Down in El Valle. That's where we're supposed to meet Hunter if we run into trouble. There's a little outdoor bar, a hut, really. He'll be there at noon every day in case we show." He met Kate's gaze, and worry hung on her face. "This will come in handy there."

Dean grabbed the black wand in his bag, toggling it on, and turned as he tossed it to his brother.

Instinctively, Lucas caught it. The wand emitted a series of high-pitched beeps.

Lucas gave a tight smile before he drew his gun on Dean. "You got me there. That was slick." He threw the wand across the room, where it clattered against the wall.

"What's going on?" Kate asked near the tail of the plane.

"Lucas has a transmitter on him. I'm betting there's audio and visual. Am I right?"

"You are correct."

"What?" Kate asked, striding back toward them. "I don't understand."

"Stay there, honey," Dean said. "Lucas isn't here to help me get away from the kill team. He's working with them. They've been listening and watching everything."

"No." Kate blanched. "That can't be."

"I'm afraid it is." Lucas tapped a button on his collar with his free hand. "They'll be here soon."

Dean was counting on it. "Why would you do this? Are you really that mad at me?"

"Mad?" Lucas scoffed. "I'm not five, having a temper tantrum. I'm furious. You left me there, knowing that I would be the sole focus of that man's violence. Left me when you could've taken me with you. Mom was already sick. She just hadn't said anything. When she started chemo, I was the one to take care of her, watched her waste away, unable to hold anything down, wondering if the treatments would kill her before the cancer. I had to go through that alone. Because you only cared about yourself. So I'm looking out for myself now."

Dean raised his palms and walked up to his brother. "Does that include killing me?"

"You don't think I can do it?" Lucas asked with the muzzle pointed at Dean's chest.

Honestly, Dean didn't know.

"You're a traitor to your country, a disgrace to the Delgado name and nothing more than a target to me."

"If that's true, then pull the trigger."

"Lucas, what are you doing?" Kate asked. "Lower the gun."

"I'm sorry, Kate. But they're almost here now."

"We're leaving," Dean said. "The only way to stop me is to shoot me."

"I can't let you leave. I have to show them I'm nothing like you. That I'm loyal to my country and to the CIA." Lucas began tightening his finger on the trigger. At the last second, he aimed for Dean's leg and pulled the trigger.

A gunshot cracked.

"No!" Kate shrieked.

Lucas's gaze dropped to the gun.

"I loaded it with blanks." Dean launched a fist to his face, propelling him back, and threw a foot to his gut.

The breath left Lucas in an explosive bark, his mouth clutching for air. Before his brother recovered, Dean got off a roundhouse kick that was a strike of force to his head and sent him spinning.

He swept up behind his brother and whipped an arm around his neck, clamping tight over his windpipe and blocking the blood flow to the brain to knock him out.

But Lucas fought back, stomping on Dean's foot and thrashing side to side to get him off balance.

"I'm sorry," Dean said to him. "I never should've left you behind."

Lucas twisted and kicked and bucked. Threw an elbow repeatedly into Dean's side.

Much more of that and Lucas would free himself or break Dean's ribs before it was lights out.

"EpiPen!" he called to Kate, and she started moving, slowly, like she was in shock. Keeping the hold locked in place, Dean wrestled him to the ground and wrapped his legs around his brother's. "You were my best friend," he said to Lucas. "It was selfish of me to go. I should have apologized. I should've begged for your forgiveness." Guilt flared up in Dean, scouring his insides, threatening to consume him. "I should've been there for you. For Mom. I love you, Lucas. You're my brother. One day, I'll earn your forgiveness. I swear it."

Kate dropped beside him. Her face was flushed and streaked with tears.

"Stick him with it," Dean said.

She popped the top and stuck the injector in Lucas's arm.

The fight was petering out of his brother; his body was growing slack. "Track...tracker," he muttered, raising his hand, but then his eyelids fluttered closed, and he went limp.

"I found the tracker on the car." Dean maintained the pressure until he was sure Lucas was out.

Kate hunched over, her shoulders shuddering. "I can't believe he was going to betray you. Shoot you."

"I can, and I knew you had to see it for yourself. But there's no time to discuss it now." Dean popped the button that Lucas had indicated as the transmitter and tossed it. Then he picked up his brother in a fireman's carry and hustled outside.

Too late.

A dark SUV was racing down the only road in or out, kicking up dust, headed straight for the hangar. The kill team would breach in less than sixty seconds.

They hurried back into the hangar.

"Grab our bags," he said to her. His sat phone was inside, and he'd need it to rendezvous with Hunter.

Kate got both their bags.

"Take my backup gun." Dean led the way through the hangar, carrying his brother into the adjacent office building.

She dug in his bag and grabbed the other nine-millimeter.

Dean moved to a far wall, putting as much distance as possible between them and the plane rigged with explosives. He dropped his brother on the floor and rushed over to the reception desk. It was beaten-up and dented, but it was sturdy.

Shoving the desk, he pushed it to the corner where Kate was huddled beside Lucas. That should provide sufficient cover from the blast.

Opening the flip phone, he heard the creak of the rusty hinges that carried with the hangar's acoustics. The team was inside.

It was time.

As he dialed the number, a shadow moved along the exterior of the building. A lone gunman crept around the office building.

Dean pointed him out to Kate and gestured for her to remain quiet.

She gave a quick nod.

Dean withdrew his gun from his pocket. Once that guy walked through the door, he'd spot them. But Dean would have to deal with him after the explosion.

He hit the call button and braced with Kate for the blast to come.

But there was no big boom, and the merc was already at the door.

What the hell?

Had the wires on the bomb loosened? He hadn't checked it in over a week.

The doorknob turned.

Dean leaped out from behind the desk, his adrenaline demanding he play offense, and charged. Just as he reached the man, the explosives detonated. The shock wave from the blast launched both men into the air and sent them tumbling outside.

The breath was knocked from Dean. Debris rained down around him. He tasted dirt and Sheetrock dust. A steady ringing filled his ears, and his body ached. His head throbbed. With his vision clearing, he pressed his palms to the ground, trying to shake the fog clouding his brain.

His hands were empty.

His weapon.

Where was his gun?

Several feet away, the other man stood and staggered, recovering faster.

Dean scanned the ground quickly. Spotted his weapon. But it wasn't within reach, and the other guy was too far away to tackle.

The merc swung his gun toward Dean, taking aim at his head.

Dean stiffened in expectation of the pain to follow.

A gun went off, and for a split second no one moved.

There was no pain as Dean sucked in a breath. Then blood spurted from a wound just above the merc's bulletproof vest below his throat. A gurgling sound came from him, and he dropped and keeled over dead.

Dean spun around on his knees to see Kate. She stood in the doorway, holding his backup weapon.

She'd saved his life. In more ways than one.

The air rushed out of his lungs in relief, his heart hammering at his chest. He crawled to his weapon, scooped it up and hauled himself to Kate. She yanked him into her arms, pressing her face to his chest. He held her tight in return, but only for a moment.

"I need to make sure the others are dead. Stay low behind the desk."

"Okay."

They both moved, separating.

He hustled back toward the hangar, taking care not to make a sound along the way. There was nothing left of the plane besides scraps of flaming metal. The wall that had been closest to the aircraft had been reduced to rubble.

Two bodies lay in close proximity to the debris. Killed by the blast.

A third man had taken a large piece of metal to a leg. It must have severed the femoral artery, from the amount of blood that had poured from his thigh. If he were unconscious and not dead, he soon would be.

Dean swept the perimeter outside to be sure he hadn't missed any others. Finally determining that the coast was clear, he made his way back to the office building.

Kate was waiting with the gun at the ready, prepared to shoot if he had been the enemy.

This time he was the one to rope her into his arms. Her body felt so good, so right against his. He let his eyes close in gratitude as he held her.

"I'm sorry for forcing you to take Lucas with us."

"It's okay. It needed to play out. You needed to see it." And Dean had needed to apologize. To tell his brother he loved him. Still.

Too bad he hadn't done it sooner. Maybe this whole thing could have been avoided.

"What are we going to do about him?" she asked, looking at Lucas.

"Nothing. He'll be out for hours. By the time he wakes, we'll be long gone." One day, Dean would clear his name, and once he did, he'd find a way to make things right with Lucas.

"I came so close to losing you," she whispered, tightening her hold on him.

"But you didn't." He looked down at her, and she met his gaze. He could see the pure love shining bright in her eyes. His world, once so dark and cold, was filled with light that warmed his heart, because he'd finally gotten the one thing he needed.

He had Kate. With her he'd found more than he ever thought possible, and he was willing to fight through anything to make sure they never lost it again.

"What do we do now?" she asked.

"Now, I make a phone call and find out where we're really going. Hopefully it's not the North Pole."

"It doesn't matter where we end up. Could be the North Pole for all I care, as long as I'll have you to keep me warm."

He dragged a hand through her hair and cupped her face. "Well, that I can guarantee. We'll be together, I'll keep you warm and we'll be safe."

Epilogue

Three weeks later

As the small motorboat pulled up to the dock for the island off the coast of Venezuela, Kate's nerves pinged to life. It was silly for her to be anxious. This was friendly territory. Nonetheless, she was, despite the vacation-like atmosphere of calm water and a balmy breeze.

In the waning light of dusk, there wasn't much she could make out on the beach besides a white house with a wraparound porch. Light shone through every window, almost as if in welcome of their arrival. Palm trees stood as a dense backdrop. Three huts were farther down the coast, but each was dark, and she couldn't see much else.

The boat stopped with the engine idling.

"Thank you," Dean said to the driver, an older woman wearing a plain blue bucket hat with a chin strap.

Every one of their contacts along their journey had worn some variation of a blue hat.

Kate thanked her as well, and the woman tipped her head in response.

Grabbing their one consolidated bag, Dean climbed out on to the dock. He took Kate's hand and helped her from the boat.

Her stomach bubbled with nerves. Their final destination had been shrouded in mystery the entire journey. Every step of the way it had been cloak and dagger. But not dangerous. If anything, it had felt *normal*, doing things other couples took for granted. Talking for hours. Sharing meals. Playing cards. Making love.

They hadn't had much access to television, but they had caught the breaking news in Wyoming. The FBI had shut down a major drug operation and prostitution ring in Albany County. Renee Olson and the second circuit judge had been arrested along with several of their associates, and the governor was under investigation. Cheryl's baby had been placed with relatives in another state. The district attorney was looking at further possible corruption among law enforcement throughout the county and had appointed a new acting sheriff.

By the time it was safe for her to go home, they had finally arrived here. On this island. She had no desire to go back, only forward, with Dean. The love of her life.

Dean had told her countless stories about Team Topaz and the members during the trip. She knew Hunter Wright would be waiting for them. That his team leader was as intrepid as he was intelligent and had come up with this last-resort measure. Each story about him had been grander and more impressive than the last. Other than that, she didn't really know what to expect from Hunter. A legend in the flesh? Or a man?

Interlacing their fingers, Kate and Dean walked hand in hand up the beach. Flowers planted around the white house saturated the air with a sultry fragrance.

"There's no reason to be nervous," Dean said in a gentle tone.

"Is it that obvious?"

He tipped his head to one side, and his mouth hitched in a playful smile. A mouth that was sexy as sin. A mouth she longed to kiss, to taste.

"Only to me. So you can relax," he said, making her smile.

"Are you sure Hunter won't have a problem with me being here, a candy-coated civilian?"

They chuckled in unison, but the sound coming from him was heavy and warm, like a hot summer night.

When he had called her *candy-coated*, she'd been livid. Hurt. Far from amused. But looking back on it, through the lens of everything they'd endured, she could laugh with ease.

"I take that back," he said. "Never should've said such a thing. Even when we were little, you were tough as nails, and you've proven you're closer to Kevlar-coated these days. But still delectably sweet on the inside." He squeezed his fingers tight around hers.

It was incredible how when they were teenagers he'd once been the center of her world. Then he'd left, taking a piece of her heart with him. She never thought she'd see him again. And now he was a pillar of support and love she couldn't imagine living without.

"Thank you," she said.

"For what?"

"For coming back to Laramie."

"I guess, technically, I came back twice. Since I crossed the state line before turning around the second time." He stopped walking and tugged her closer, bringing them chest to chest, and held her against him in a warm embrace. "I came back for you. I'm sorry it took you being in danger and nearly dying for me to see it.

Not sure how I missed the obvious before. I've never gotten over you."

Staring up at him, she basked in the look in his eyes, in the sincerity of his words that resonated deep in her bones, in how he made her feel strong and delicate and beautiful at the same time.

She ran her hand through his cool, dark hair. The longer curls at the front had that enticing windblown look you'd only see in a commercial or magazine ad.

"I'm not sorry," she said. Not one bit. "Everything that happened brought us back together. Brought us here, where we'll be safe. And it made you realize you love me."

Lowering his head, he trailed a path of kisses from her temple to her jaw. His beard brushed her cheek, his stubble a titillating scrape against her skin, sending a shiver of delight down her spine. "I've loved you since I was fifteen. Always have and always will. Not a day has gone by when that one thing wasn't true."

Her heart hung suspended a moment and then beat again hard. She believed him, without a doubt in her mind. "I love you, too," she said, not a canned response but the unvarnished truth.

She pressed her palms to his cheeks, drawing his full lips to hers, and gave him a greedy, needful kiss. He slid his hand beneath her hair, his thumb stroking the back of her neck, his fingers tightening on her nape. She breathed him in, savoring the taste of him.

Her knees weakened, and when he drew back, they came apart breathless.

He flashed her one of those grins that was loaded with sensual promise. "If you keep that up, we'll never make it inside."

If she weren't concerned about being a rude guest as well as an uninvited one, she would've dragged Dean down the beach and had her way with him.

"All right, let's go, but I have plans for you later," she said, thinking of how she'd worship his hot, muscled body with her mouth.

"I'm going to hold you to that."

"I would hope for nothing less." She gave him a devilish wink.

Another hearty chuckle rolled from his lips. He dropped his arms from around her and took her hand. As they strolled up to the house, she felt lighter, less worried.

The front door opened before they hit the stairs. A guy dressed in khaki shorts and a T-shirt stepped out onto the porch. "I see you made it."

"Hunter," Dean said with a smile.

A couple of inches taller than Dean, tanned and sculpted, Hunter was a rather perfect specimen of a man, like Brad Pitt at any age. But she guessed Hunter was in his mid-to-late forties.

They walked up the steps.

Dean shook Hunter's hand, and the greeting quickly turned into a one-armed hug.

"This is Kate Sawyer."

"Ah," Hunter said with a raise of his eyebrows and a knowing grin, as though he'd heard her name before. "It's a pleasure to meet you, notwithstanding the circumstances."

Up close under a porch light, he was almost impossibly handsome. Smiling blue eyes that drew you in and golden-blond hair that didn't come from a bottle. But Dean was far more alluring in a dark, magnetic way. Or perhaps it was her hormones talking.

Hunter took her hand in a warm, firm grip. "I hope the trip wasn't too difficult. I'm sorry it was so long, but a necessary precaution."

"The trip was fine." Her smile was shaky as fresh nerves fluttered in her stomach. "No complaints." As long as she was with Dean, nothing else mattered.

Laughter came from the back of the house. Several voices.

Dean looked toward the screen door. "Who's here?"

"I've got a full house."

A bright smile stretched across Dean's face, but surprise lit up his brown eyes. "Zee and Gage are here?"

Kate didn't think she'd get the chance to meet Zenobia Hanley, hacker extraordinaire, and Gage Graham, *cleanup* specialist. If she understood correctly, Gage made dead bodies disappear or could make a government assassination look like an accident.

Over the years, they had become more than his friends. They were Dean's family.

"Gage came in first," Hunter said, slipping his hands in his pockets. "He brought Hope Fischer with him. She's a photojournalist. He saved her life and helped her track down her sister's murderer. Somewhere along the way they fell in love. Next was Zee. She's here with Olivia and her fiancé, John Lowry."

"Who's Olivia?" Kate asked.

"Her daughter," both men said at the same time.

"She's eleven," Hunter added.

"Did Zee get engaged while on the run?" Dean asked.

"No. John proposed here on the beach a few weeks ago. With everyone showing up with a significant other, I'm thinking about dubbing this place Love Island."

"Oh, man," Dean said with a shake of his head and a chuckle. "I missed a lot."

"You have no idea. Hope is pregnant."

Dean rocked back on his heels. "Wow."

"Gage still doesn't know. Zee does. I think John might, too. But don't say anything. It's Hope's place to tell him."

"Why hasn't she?" Kate asked, and Hunter gave her a strange look she couldn't decipher. Maybe the team of superspies was used to keeping secrets, but if they'd been a bunch of civilians, someone would've let the news slip by now. "Not that I'm judging. Or trying to stick my nose in where it doesn't belong."

"Every time Hope mentions babies," Hunter said, "Gage talks about how he doesn't want to be a father. I think she's scared and still processing everything. When the time is right, she'll tell him. Or she'll start showing and he'll figure it out."

Dean snickered. "I can't wait to catch up with everyone."

"Follow me." Hunter opened the door and led the way into the house.

As the door closed behind them, a series of low beeps chimed. Hunter and Dean turned toward the sound.

Mounted on the wall beside the door was a rectangular black device with two antennae at the top. An LED display across the front panel had an illuminated bar of green and orange lights.

Dean and Hunter exchanged a look, their faces impassive, but there was a sudden DEFCON 1 high-alert tension swelling in the room.

"What is that?" Kate asked.

Hunter's gaze slid to her. "In laymen's terms, a bug detector."

"It'll ping from any analog, digital, GSM cellular or Wi-Fi-based listening and tracking devices within forty feet," Dean said.

"Did you bring cell phones with you?" Hunter asked Dean.

"Come on, I'm not stupid."

"All right. The two of you stand at least ten feet apart." Hunter grabbed the device from the wall.

Dean extended his arms and spread his legs. Kate did likewise.

First Hunter waved the black device around Dean's head, over his arms, down his torso, in between his legs and across his boots. Then repeated the procedure along his backside, taking particular care with their bag.

Nothing.

Kate gulped. "Maybe the equipment is faulty."

"It's not," Hunter said with sharp finality and turned to her. His jaw was hard, his eyes narrowed in suspicion as he raised the device in front of her.

Beeps pinged, and the LED lights flashed from orange to red.

Kate shook her head. There had to be a mistake. "I don't understand."

Hunter's gaze swung to Dean. "Who would know to plant a tracker on her instead of you?"

Dean clenched his hand in a fist and lowered his head. "Lucas. The agency sent him after me. I made the mistake of letting him get too close. It almost cost me my life." He looked up at Hunter. "I'm sorry. I've put everyone in jeopardy by coming here."

"No, I did. This is my fault," Kate said. "You asked

me to keep an eye on Lucas when you left the two of us alone. He got me to lower my defenses, to remember how close we once were, how he used to be." A lost little boy who had missed his brother as much as she did. The two of them struggling and lonely, clinging to each other to get through it. "Then he brought up the kidnapping and encouraged me to take a shower. That getting cleaned up would make me feel better. And like a fool, I did." She could kick herself. If only she'd had the common sense to mention it to Dean, they could've avoided this doomsday scenario. "Lucas had access to my things, and when I came out of the bathroom, he had fresh clothes for me in his hands. I never thought anything of it. It didn't occur to me that he'd plant a tracker on me."

Although it should've. Lucas had turned into a 007 operative, as slick and deadly as Dean. If one of them was capable of wearing a realistic disguise, passing himself off as another person for months, why wouldn't the other be capable of embedding a tracker in her clothes?

"You are *not* going to take this on your shoulders." Dean clutched her arms. "I should've checked our things. This is on me."

"Yes. It is." Hunter's tone was matter-of-fact. "If I had to venture a guess, I'd say the tracker was in your bra. Dean, check for it." Hunter turned around, facing the door.

That's where it had to be. Once they'd reached a warmer climate, she'd picked up shorts, tank tops, a couple of sundresses. The only thing she had no need to replace were her undergarments.

Kate unclasped her bra, slipped her arms through the straps, pulled it from her tank top and handed to Dean. Not bothering with the straps or clasp, he inspected the seam of her underwire. A hole had been made. One she hadn't noticed. Manipulating the material with his fingers, he pulled out a filament-thin device and gave her bra back.

"GPS tracking only," Dean said.

While he showed Hunter, she stepped into a corner and quickly put her bra on.

"Very clever of Lucas." It almost sounded like admiration in Hunter's tone.

"He's on Cinnabar now. I found out Butch is his team leader."

"I bet this was Butch's idea. In case you gave him the slip, he could still locate you."

"Us. They want the whole team."

Kate rejoined them.

"Please tell me you at least got something useful out of Lucas," Hunter said.

"You won't want to hear it."

"When did *want* ever factor into this? If you've learned something, I *need* to know."

"The reason everyone believes we're traitors is because there's a money trail. A half million dollars in offshore accounts for all of us. Deposited two days before the mission."

"I'm aware of that already. Zee told me when she arrived. She found out through tracking Bertrand's research. Is there anything else?"

Dean took a deep breath. "I don't know for certain who set us up, but… Kelly Russell was promoted."

Hunter staggered back a couple of steps, as though he'd been physically hit. "Promoted?"

"To deputy director of operations."

Hunter's jaw dropped.

Kate recalled a similar look of shock on Dean's face and what he'd said to Lucas.

She didn't get fired or quit in outrage over the injustice of what happened?

Kate supposed the same thing must have been going through Hunter's mind. She didn't fully grasp what it meant to be a team's handler, but she understood that complete trust was required for a successful mission. Every time a team went out, their lives were in the hands of their handler.

If this Kelly Russell had been the one to set up Team Topaz, then it was the greatest betrayal imaginable. Though what Lucas had pulled was a close second.

Hunter was standing stock-still, looking at the floor or perhaps nothing at all, almost in a daze.

Dean drew closer to him, slowly, as if approaching a deadly predator. "Hunter?" he asked in a tentative tone. "Are you all right?"

"Surprised." Hunter gave a tiny shake of his head and schooled his features into a blank canvas. "That's all."

From everything Dean had shared, that was a lot. It took something colossal to surprise the great Hunter Wright.

"Kelly could be coldhearted for sure, a royal pain at times," Hunter said. "But always a consummate professional. I didn't take her for a backstabbing opportunist." A spark of emotion flashed across his face.

Kate would've sworn it was pain. That the news of their handler had wounded him.

"Do you think she was the one who set us up?" Dean asked.

"I don't know. But I intend to find out. The one thing that's now certain is she benefited."

Jubilant voices and more laughter came from the back patio, drawing their gazes.

"They're playing Dungeons and Dragons Adventure Begins," Hunter said in a low, despondent voice. "We're all hooked."

The rest of his team had found a sanctuary here. They were couples in love, engaged, pregnant, with an eleven-year-old to boot, outside laughing, playing normal games. And her arrival with Dean put everything and everyone in jeopardy. The entire house of cards was about to come tumbling down around them.

Kate fought to tamp down the nausea rising in her stomach.

"What are we going to do about the GPS tracker?" Dean asked.

"Absolutely nothing. If we destroy it, they'll know we found it. I'll put it on one of my garments to keep it moving."

"So we just leave it?" Kate asked, stunned. "And wait for a kill team to come?"

"Precisely." Hunter's tone was cool and nonchalant.

Way too cool and far too nonchalant to give Kate the slightest chance at having peace of mind. How could he consider that to be a plan, much less a good one?

Dean had raved about Hunter being a master strategist. Well, this was hardly convincing evidence.

"I've been expecting this," Hunter said. "Not the GPS tracker per se, but with the entire team needing to punch out of wherever they'd been lying low and coming here, it was only a matter of time before the CIA found us. This can work out in our favor. Now we have a better timeline of when they'll get here. Once they do, they'll do recon before they strike. Since they don't know that we know they're coming, we'll have the tactical advantage."

"Dean." Kate turned to him with her heart in her throat. "You said sticking around with a kill team on the way was suicide."

"I did say that. But we got out of Laramie, didn't we?"

"Barely." They'd almost died. More than once.

Dean curled his hands around her shoulders and rubbed up and down her arms. "We need to trust Hunter. He knows what he's doing."

"I've given every scenario considerable thought," Hunter said. "And discussed it with the others. John had some good ideas."

"Is John in our line of business?" Dean asked.

"In a manner of speaking, he used to be. Navy SEAL."

"Aha." Dean nodded like that explained everything.

What was wrong with these two? Why weren't they panicking? How could they act so cavalier?

"Isn't this island the end of the road?" Kate asked. "As in there's nowhere else to run. Nowhere else to hide."

"That's right." Hunter's tone was all easy-breezy. "Our time on Love Island has come to an end."

"But we just got here," she said, realizing the words had been uttered out loud and not in her head. In a voice that bordered on whiny, no less.

"Team Topaz is done running." Hunter caught her gaze as he spoke. "We're done hiding. We need to figure out who put us in this predicament and fight back."

"Fight?" Kate was suddenly dizzy. She thought she'd left the fighting behind in Wyoming. "I'm not a warrior. Or a superagent. I'm a veterinarian, for crying out loud." She breathed through the panic attempting to burrow its way into her mind.

"Oh, good." Hunter nodded in approval. "We could use a doctor."

She treated animals. *Not people!* It wasn't the same thing.

Kate wrapped her arms around her midsection. "I think I'm going to be sick." Once again, she'd meant to keep that to herself, but it just kept slipping out.

"The bathroom is right down the hall." Hunter pointed. "I hope you'll still be up to eating. It was my turn to cook family night dinner. I made *hallacas*. Corn dough wrapped in plantain, filled with beef, olives, pork, capers and a few veggies. Not to toot my own horn, but they're pretty delicious. Even Olivia raved about them. There's some grilled meat and fish as well in case you don't do carbs."

The glorious days when not eating carbs actually occurred to her.

Their nights of playing games and enjoying family dinners—another ordinary thing under extraordinary circumstances—were numbered thanks to her.

The situation was dire, and she was at fault, regardless of what Dean had told her, but she didn't want to give Hunter the wrong impression. To have him thinking she wasn't up for this, couldn't cut it. That she was candy-coated. Worse, she didn't want him to assume she regretted her decision to come here.

Given the chance to do it all over again, she would still choose Dean every single time. No matter the consequences.

"We'll be okay." Dean slipped a comforting arm around her shoulders, tucking her against his side. "We'll get through this. We've got the whole team and a SEAL."

Swallowing against the fear pooling in her gut, she

leaned into his strong frame, absorbed his body heat and hopefully a fraction of his confidence. "I know. It's just…" Hauling in a deep breath, she calmed her mind to get the words right. "I wasn't prepared for this."

Therein lay the problem, the difference between her and the two formidable, unfazed men in the room. They were highly skilled, hardened professionals who had been trained for this. Who lived and breathed it. Danger was nothing new to them. Fighting was second nature.

"Look on the bright side," Hunter said. "At least you're not unprepared *and* pregnant."

Poor Hope. Here Kate was feeling sorry for herself, wallowing in fear when she didn't have nearly as much to contend with as Hope. Or the eleven-year-old, for that matter. Both civilians, unaccustomed to this crazy 007 lifestyle.

Although she hadn't met Hope yet, she was important to Gage, who was like a brother to Dean. That made her important to Kate. The same went for Olivia and John.

She needed to be strong, put on a brave face, not only to alleviate Dean's concerns, but because others were going to need her. They were all in this together.

Buck up. You've got this.

"You're right," Kate said to Hunter. He had a remarkable way of putting things into focus, showing her where she needed to concentrate her energy. "It was selfish to only think of myself and how this affects me."

"Not selfish. Only human. Don't beat yourself up over it. I was only trying to lighten the mood."

More like trying to lighten *her* mood. She was the only one acting as if the apocalypse was imminent while Dean was composed and Hunter was talking about *hallacas* and Dungeons and Dragons.

She needed a mental course correction. To do a complete one-eighty.

Hunter looked at Dean. "You've got a good one. A keeper. But I'm sure you already know that."

"Yeah, I do." Dean's arm tightened around her. "Would you give us a minute before we head out back to see the others?"

"Sure. Take all the time you need. I'll get them up to speed on the latest developments." He gave Dean a pat on the back and left them alone in the foyer. "Hey." He turned her to face him and met her eyes. "It's a lot to take in, especially after I promised you that we'd be safe here. Are you all right?"

She took his hands in hers and stepped in between his spread feet, getting closer. "I had no idea what I was capable of, how strong I could be, until you came back home."

"Until I put you in harm's way, you mean."

"You didn't send Cheryl to me. You didn't put that thumb drive in my pocket. You didn't encourage me to get to the bottom of what was going on. In fact, you did the opposite, trying to protect me. You didn't put me in danger, Dean. I did that, all by myself." She sucked in a shaky breath. But because of Dean, everything had worked out. "I'm not going to lie, I'm scared. But I can face this. With you."

He stroked her hair and cupped her face, caressing her cheek with his thumb. His touch soothed something deep inside her, quelling her nerves, her fears.

"You're not angry," he said in a low, soft voice, "that I broke my promise, albeit inadvertently, about coming here and being safe?"

"We'd be in danger no matter where we ended up

thanks to Lucas's tracker." *Sneaky devil.* Instead of kicking herself, she wanted to kick him. "This is the best place for us. It'll be easier to survive here than on our own. One team, one fight. And we've got a SEAL." She summoned a smile, for him.

He took her face between both his hands and stared into her eyes. "You're incredible."

When he looked at her like that, she felt incredible. Like together anything was possible. And she believed they'd not only get through this, but on the other side of it, they'd be even closer. More grateful for this precious love.

"You're not too shabby, either," she said.

He grinned, and she found herself laughing. Even though they weren't safe and soon they'd be thrust into the fray again, this amazing man made the ugliness and violence fade to the background. Just with a smile and brush of his hand.

Dean pressed his lips to hers in a tender kiss. "If you're not ready to meet everyone, they'll understand. It can wait until morning."

"Are you kidding me? After all the stories you told me about them for weeks, I'm champing at the bit." He must've been ten times as eager, and she wouldn't delay the reunion. Besides, tucking her tail and scurrying off would send the wrong message. Not only to Hunter, but to all of them. "I want to meet your family. The people who are going to be my family, too."

"I'm so lucky to have you." He took her hand, and they strolled through the house toward the open door that led to the patio, but they couldn't see anyone from the hall.

"I hope they like me." As silly as it seemed, their approval meant something to her.

"Don't worry," he whispered. "They're going to love you."

"How do you know?"

"Because I love you. They'll bend over backward and sideways, contorting themselves into pretzels to make you feel accepted."

Laughing softly, she followed him across the threshold and into the sweet night air.

They were greeted with bright smiles, arms extended in welcome and an overwhelming atmosphere of joy.

Dean started the flurry of introductions in between hugs.

From the way he had talked about Zee, Kate had discerned that the hotshot computer whiz easily garnered male attention. So, naturally, Kate had expected her to be beautiful, but the woman was downright stunning. Flawless light brown skin, long spiral curls and every inch of her body was lean and toned, yet feminine. Zee's daughter, Olivia, was a mini version of her. There was a rugged handsomeness to John. Everything about him was strong—his features, his build, his presence. It was plain to see that Zee and John were madly in love and couldn't keep their hands off each other.

Gage was quiet yet friendly. Kept a low profile, hovering in the background. Despite the fact he was no less good-looking than the others, something about him gave Kate the impression that he was the type who could blend in most places or could slip away without anyone noticing.

Except for Hope. She'd notice.

Pretty in a girl-next-door way, she had intelligent eyes

and radiated a warmth that drew you in. Made it easy to be in her orbit.

Every member of Team Topaz, including John—a de facto member—had a different physique, yet they all carried themselves the same. With a lethal readiness.

She had no doubt their skills were as deadly as Dean's.

Once the greetings were finished, she thought they'd launch into strategy mode, start planning their next move in light of the GPS tracker Hunter had found on her.

Instead, the conversation stayed casual and buoyant, as one would expect at a family reunion.

Dean dropped into a lounge chair and pulled her down onto his lap, slipping an arm around her shoulders and the other across her thighs.

Letting herself relax, she nestled against him.

He tipped his head back and glanced up at her. When their gazes met, he smiled and mouthed, "You're so beautiful."

She grinned from ear to ear, her cheeks heating, her heart filled to bursting with love for him. In the days ahead, no matter what they had to face, they'd do it together. Because what they shared, what they'd found, was worth any fight.

* * * * *

Look for the next title in the Fugitive Heroes:
Topaz Unit series by Juno Rushdan
wherever Harlequin Books are sold.

Previous titles include:
Rogue Christmas Operation
Alaskan Christmas Escape
Disavowed in Wyoming

Coming next month:
An Operative's Last Stand

#2049 MURDER ON PRESCOTT MOUNTAIN
A Tennessee Cold Case Story by Lena Diaz

Former soldier Grayson Prescott started his cold case firm to bring murderers to justice—specifically the one who destroyed his life. When his obsession intersects with Detective Willow McCray's serial killer investigation, they join forces to stop the mounting danger. Catching the River Road rapist will save the victims...but will it save their future together?

#2050 CONSPIRACY IN THE ROCKIES
Eagle Mountain: Search for Suspects • by Cindi Myers

The grisly death of a prominent rancher stuns a Colorado community and plunges Deputy Chris Delray into a murder investigation. He teams up with Willow Russell, the victim's fiery daughter, to discover her father's enemies. But when Willow becomes a target, Chris suspects her conspiracy theory might be right—and larger than they ever imagined...

#2051 GRAVE DANGER
Defenders of Battle Mountain • by Nichole Severn

When a young woman is discovered buried alive, Colorado ME Dr. Chloe Pascale knows that the relentless serial killer she barely escaped has found her. To stop him, she must trust police chief Weston Ford with her darkest secrets. But getting too close is putting their guarded hearts at risk—and leading into an inescapable trap...

#2052 AN OPERATIVE'S LAST STAND
Fugitive Heroes: Topaz Unit • by Juno Rushdan

Barely escaping CIA mercenaries, ex-agent Hunter Wright is after the person who targeted his ops team, Topaz, for treason. Deputy director Kelly Russell is convinced Hunter went rogue. But now she's his only shot at getting the answers they need. Can they trust each other enough to save Topaz—and each other?

#2053 JOHN DOE COLD CASE
A Procedural Crime Story • by Amanda Stevens

The discovery of skeletal remains in a Florida cavern sends cold case detective Eve Jareau on a collision course with her past. Concealing the truth from her boss, police chief Nash Bowden, becomes impossible when the killer, hell-bent on keeping decades-old family secrets hidden, is lying in wait...to bury Eve and Nash alive.

#2054 RESOLUTE JUSTICE
by Leslie Marshman

Between hunting human traffickers and solving her father's murder, Sheriff Cassie Reed has her hands full. So finding charming PI Tyler Bishop's runaway missing niece isn't a priority—especially when he won't stop breaking the rules. But when a leak in her department brings Cassie under suspicion, joining forces with the tantalizing rebel is her only option.

*When a young woman is discovered buried alive,
Colorado ME Dr. Chloe Pascale knows that the
relentless serial killer she barely escaped has found her.
To stop him, she must trust police chief
Weston Ford with her darkest secrets. But getting
too close is putting their guarded hearts at risk—and
leading into an inescapable trap...*

*Read on for a sneak preview of
Grave Danger,
part of the Defenders of Battle Mountain series
from Nichole Severn.*

Three months ago...
When I'm done, you're going to beg me for the pain.

Chloe Pascale struggled to open her eyes. She blinked against
the brightness of the sky. Trees. Snow. Cold. Her head pounded in
rhythm to her racing heartbeat. Shuffling reached her ears as her
last memories lightninged across her mind like a half-remembered
dream. She'd gone out for a run on the trail near her house. Then...
Fear clawed at her insides, her hands curling into fists. He'd come
out of the woods. He'd... She licked her lips, her mouth dry. He'd
drugged her, but with what and how many milliliters, she wasn't
sure. The haze of unconsciousness slipped from her mind, and a
new terrifying reality forced her from ignorance. "Where am I?"

Dead leaves crunched off to her left. Her attacker's dark outline
shifted in her peripheral vision. Black ski mask. Lean build. Tall.
Well over six feet. Unfamiliar voice. Black jeans. His knees popped
as he crouched beside her, the long shovel in his left hand digging

into the soil near her head. The tip of the tool was coated in mud. Reaching a gloved hand toward her, he stroked the left side of her jawline, ear to chin, and a shiver chased down her spine against her wishes. "Don't worry, Dr. Miles. It'll all be over soon."

His voice… It sounded…off. Disguised?

"How do you know my name? What do you want?" She blinked to clear her head. The injection site at the base of her neck itched, then burned, and she brought her hands up to assess the damage. Ropes encircled her wrists, and she lifted her head from the ground. Her ankles had been bound, too. She pulled against the strands, but she couldn't break through. Then, almost as though demanding her attention, she caught sight of the refrigerator. Old. Light blue. Something out of the '50s with curves and heavy steel doors.

"I know everything about you, Chloe. Can I call you Chloe?" he asked. "I know where you live. I know where you work. I know your running route and how many hours you spend at the clinic. You really should change up your routine. Who knows who could be out there watching you? As for what I want, well, I'm going to let you figure that part out once you're inside."

Pressure built in her chest. She dug her heels into the ground, but the soil only gave way. No. No, no, no, no. This wasn't happening. Not to her. Darkness closed in around the edges of her vision, her breath coming in short bursts. Pulling at the ropes again, she locked her jaw against the scream working up her throat. She wasn't going in that refrigerator like the other victim she'd heard about on the news. Dr. Roberta Ellis. Buried alive, killed by asphyxiation. Tears burned in her eyes as he straightened and turned his back to her to finish the work he'd started with the shovel.

Don't miss
Grave Danger *by Nichole Severn,*
available February 2022 wherever
Harlequin books and ebooks are sold.

Harlequin.com